THE GOLD PERSIMMON

THE GOLD PERSIMMON

LINDSAY MERBAUM

Creature Publishing
Brooklyn, NY

Creature Publishing and logo are registered trademarks of
Creature Publishing, LLC.

Spine illustration and cover design by Rachel Kelli
Distribution through Ingram

ISBN 978-1-951971-05-2
LCCN 2021930862

CREATUREHORROR.COM
🐦 @creaturelit
📷 @creaturepublishing

For all the teachers who humored my stubbornness,
nourished my curiosity and, above all, encouraged me
to write into the unknown.

THE GOLD PERSIMMON

I dreamt of falling trees in a wild storm
I was between them as a desolate shore
came to meet me and I ran, scared stiff,
there was a trapdoor but I could not lift it [. . .]

—*The White Hotel* by D.M. Thomas

PART I

I

The lobby is cool and quiet as a tomb, the only sound the soft burble of the fountain behind the desk: a hunk of stone with a ripple of shimmer coursing through it like a silver strand of hair, a spring pouring forth from the head, washing over the persimmon tree carved into the rockface. Green moss and tiny white flowers hide in the crevices. The orchids shiver.

Cly stands behind the desk with her hands on the poreless granite, caressing the stone. The world outside is one of car horns, garbage, cell phone chatter, the obscenity of roaring trucks, the boom and clank of construction. Inside, this is her world. When guests arrive one at a time, she studies their faces as they cross the threshold. Some of them tremble. Others smile with obvious relief, float up to the check-in desk.

"Welcome," Cly says and means it. A sleek black nametag is pinned to her cream blouse, just above her breast. Her long black hair—wavy, almost curly—is pulled back in a gold clip. She wears simple gold earrings and a matching pendant in the shape of a persimmon tree. On her desk, there is a glass bowl of persimmons. She offers one to each guest. The fruit will never go out of season. It's grown especially for the hotel in a greenhouse somewhere.

There are people who come here so their former selves can die, so they can transform into something else. Sometimes, when guests return to the lobby to check out after their stay, Cly does not recognize them. Their faces are the same, yet not. Once in a while, someone's hair goes white.

Cly doesn't know what exactly happens in those rooms because it is not her business to know. Even the guests themselves probably couldn't explain it. But she does know something about solitude, about a quiet that can be deafening. She is the priestess, offering safe passage.

When Edith arrives, Cly notes her jaunty little walk, her stylish leather jacket. She smirks and simpers, the first to survey the lobby with such obvious self-satisfaction, savoring the sight of each object—the orchids, the plush couches no one ever sits on, the fountain, even Cly herself—and finding a secret pleasure in it all.

When Edith reaches the desk, hands stuffed in her pockets, she looks Cly right in the eye and smiles. She says "Hi," slowly, with great purpose, the word accompanied by that smirk, teeth gleaming. Her voice is too loud; Cly winces.

"Welcome," she says. But this time, she does not mean it, not exactly. What she means to say is, *Are you sure this is where you're supposed to be?*

Edith looks around again. She has no luggage, just a backpack slung over one shoulder. She tosses her head and her short, fine hair falls into her eyes, then she brushes it away.

It's light brown, almost blond, with strands of silver. Her eyes, blue-gray, are framed by tentative quotation marks. Cly thinks she looks younger than she is; there are at least ten years between them.

As Cly brings up her reservation on the computer, Edith plucks a persimmon from the bowl and casually rolls it around in her hands.

Finally, it's time for the presentation of the key. She offers Edith the shining black card in her cupped palms, the way she's been taught to do, the way she's always done it.

Edith arches an eyebrow. "Really?"

Cly nods.

"Okay, then." She takes the key, allows her finger to graze Cly's palm. It's full of electricity. Zip.

"You going to be down here for a while?"

Cly pulls at her shirt, composing herself. "Yes, ma'am, until one o'clock."

Edith smirks at her again for saying *ma'am*. Then she glances at her nametag. "Well, if you want some company, you know where to find me, *Clytemnestra*." She pronounces her full name like an inside joke. With that, she saunters off toward the gilded elevator, where an attendant awaits to shuttle her to her room. She hums to herself as she goes, tosses the persimmon in the air. She catches it, throws it again, a prince with a golden bauble.

The next day, Cly finds on her desk a small piece of heavy, cream stationary, folded in half. She knows who's left it, though she plays coy with herself and pretends she doesn't. Her hands tremble as she unfolds the paper to sneak a peek, then she secrets it away in her pocket. The note contains no words of flattery. No poetry or little jokes. In fact, there are no words at all, just a phone number in neat, block letters. Such delicious arrogance, her mother might say.

After her shift ends, Cly goes home and sinks into the tub. She closes her eyes, feels again the guest's finger—Edith's— grazing her palm. In spite of herself, she imagines Edith's hands on her body, grasping, pawing. The scene is startling. Cly opens the tap to disguise the sound of the water sloshing with the movement of her hips.

Sometimes she ducks under. Even submerged, holding her breath, she can still taste her mother's cigarettes. What would it be like to experience everything like this? The sounds of the world flattened and distorted, rendered distant yet incredibly close. Cly imagines drifting up, out of her body, floating through the bathroom doorway, then to the right toward the kitchen. There, on the table, she sees her mother's notebook full of poetry she never lets anyone look at. Meanwhile, her father paces, muttering lectures to the pigeons on the windowsill. Her parents no longer sleep. They're alert, monitoring her comings and goings, waiting for her when she gets home, no matter the hour. All their friends drifted away years ago. Their own parents are dead in countries they will never see again. If Cly had the money, she would've sent them long ago to a crumbling Mediterranean villa. They would wear dark sunglasses, her mother an enormous hat, and languorously smoke long, skinny cigarettes as they lay in the shade, dying slowly in the crepuscule like old-world vampires while a servant force-fed them overripe fruit.

"How can you work at such a place? A hotel?" her mother the famed poetess says over and over, spitting the words, as if Cly is a chambermaid, cleaning toilets. It doesn't matter to Claire that only the best are selected for Check-In. Cly knows that working at a hotel isn't really what her mother objects to, anyway. That she herself in her youth cleaned houses and wore the same clothes every day so she could afford to drink espresso and write poems all night. The rules at The Gold Persimmon are what Claire can never understand or approve of. The Gold Persimmon is a precisely ordered world full of musts and musn'ts. Guests arrive at their appointed check-in desk at the mandated time, then are ushered to their cocoons for the night. They will never be encroached upon by a waiter bearing a tray, never cross paths with housekeeping's cumbersome cart in the hallway. Claire is a woman who makes a scene at every opportunity. She much prefers chaos.

All the privacy measures created a great deal of buzz when the hotel first opened. Wellness influencers and Western Buddhists penned op-eds, while magazines, newspapers, and travel sites published profiles suggesting big-name celebrities and politicians were booking rooms to grieve their divorces and lost campaigns in style. But Cly has never seen a face she recognizes. The writers who produce those articles seem to miss the point entirely: discretion is not the purpose of the hotel. The purpose of the hotel *requires* discretion.

There are rumors cameras are installed in some of the rooms. Alone at the desk at night, the other Check-In girls grow bored, uneasy. It feels like there's always someone looking over your shoulder, they say. They also claim a phantom woman runs naked through the hall on the ninth floor—the one conveniently closed for renovations. How do they know if no one goes up there?

The Accident didn't occur on the ninth floor, but the twentieth. The official story: a guest fell out a window. Unofficially: a guest became intoxicated in his room, then threw himself out the window.

When it happened, Cly was at her post awaiting the next guest, who wasn't due for another hour. The bowl of persimmons gleamed atop the desk. Behind her, the rock fountain sshhed water as the white moth orchids nodded to each other in the circulated air. She scrolled through the day's reservations, each name precious as a secret.

Then, a boom, followed by a car alarm. The lobbies, unlike the rooms, were padded but not soundproof. Cly assumed there'd been a car crash out on the street. She stared straight ahead at the tinted glass doors and waited for something to happen, for someone to come running in. Then she heard shouts followed by a scream. She rushed outside.

The body had landed on a car. The roof of the vehicle was crushed. Cly found herself standing right in front of it, though she didn't know how she'd gotten so close. The alarm whooped. She saw hair, dark hair. It was wet. There was blood on what remained of the windshield, deep in the cracks. It looked like a stained-glass window had shattered. Behind her, Duke was losing it, screaming at everyone to stay calm. Someone was crying. Sirens sounded in the distance.

Cly looked and looked. She couldn't stop: the crushed roof of the car, the windshield in pieces on the ground like shattered quartz. The back of the man's head, the hair curly, thick with black blood. His hand dangling, fingernails immaculate. The shoe on the pavement, several feet away. It was a tennis shoe, still clean and white, the kind her father would wear to go for a walk.

"All right, everybody, all right!" Duke motioned for them to follow him away from the car. The paramedics had arrived.

"This is a terrible thing, yes. But don't forget, we've still got people upstairs who have no idea what's happened, and they're gonna need to be taken care of. Get back to your stations, try to keep it together, and I'll tell you what to do as soon as I know what the fuck we're gonna do. Okay?"

No one said anything. The crying woman continued sobbing.

"For Christ sakes, get her out of here. Somebody call a sub."

The police arrived.

"Fuck," Duke said when he saw them. "Okay, people. Let's go. We've got work to do. And nobody talks to the fucking press!"

The reporters showed up later, crowding the lobbies, talking too loudly, sullying the floor with their shoes and spilled coffee, forcing Duke to rush around, herding them out of the building before any of the guests saw them. They were hoping the body belonged to someone famous. But his name wasn't one anyone had heard before.

Cly stood there. She regarded the glass, the blood on the ground, the pristine shoe, the hand, the fingers curled as if something had fallen from its grasp. She tugged at her eyelashes.

"C'mon, people, move!" Duke shouted. He was flushed and sweating.

Cly shivered but didn't think to close her arms across her chest so they hung unused at her sides as she slowly walked back to her desk. The others drifted this way and that around her, meandering toward their respective entrances.

The story was all over the news. Yet no one spoke to the press. Cly knows it wasn't so much out of loyalty to the hotel as pity for the guest: he'd lost a child, it turned out. They called it "The Accident" to refer both to the man himself and what happened to him. Clytemnestra heard that Duke went to the funeral. The staff were talking then, to anyone they could find, even Cly. They were afflicted with a kind of compulsive chattiness. Their hands shook.

Afterwards, the hotel closed for renovations. Windows were installed that couldn't be opened or broken. Alcohol was also made unavailable.

Meanwhile, Cly took an office temp job and bided her time, making copies and spreadsheets, fiddling with paperclips and rubber bands at her cubicle. Other Gold Persimmon employees found permanent jobs elsewhere, with fewer protocols and risks. But Cly went back.

"How can you go back?" her mother wanted to know.

It was not a question she'd ever considered. Of course she would return to faithfully execute her duties. There was no other path.

When they reopened after the renovations, demand surpassed what it had been before The Accident. Duke was pleased, though in those first few weeks, he darted about frantically, dark circles of sweat staining his shirt. All the returning staff were on edge, on the lookout for something, they didn't know what. An emergency team, exclusive to the hotel, remained on standby in case of incident.

The bathwater is bluish with soap, a thin, creamy film of bubbles on top. Cly skims it off with her arms and there she is beneath the water: her own legs, dark pubis. As she moves, the body follows.

She stands dripping at the sink and wipes the fog off the mirror, peers at the head inside with black hair, a face that matches her own. The old fantasy unravels itself wordlessly, pulling her into the myth of the second skin, the one she knows by heart. Already she's breathing hard.

The heat of the steam has softened the glass to gelatin. The mirror's face emerges, glistening like a birth. She's smiling. They stand lip to lip. Cly's nipples are hard. Her double is smooth and slick as water. She rubs, palms, slides her wet fingers. Cly moans. She is alive, alive. This is real. Her hipbones collide against the heavy edge of the sink as the reflection goes black. A portal, it swallows her whole.

When she's finished, there's a scratch along the edge of her lower lip, a line of blood, like lipstick applied with impossible precision. The mirror is sharp.

Cly falls asleep in her robe, her hair damp on the pillow. Tonight, she will have the dream again, the one where she's working Check-In D.

The lobby is dark, cold and moist as a cave. She sees a figure pass through the door, then come toward her, but she can't make out his face. He moves haltingly, dragging one half of his body. Slowly, he labors toward the desk where she waits with her hands folded as if in prayer. The desk is ivory. Cly notes one of the man's arms hangs loose at his side. His leg is twisted, the knee inverted. His face is smashed, the eyes drooping from the sockets, the skin torn away like a peeled peach, his teeth whitish nubs protruding from his gums.

"Good afternoon," Cly says. "What is your name?"

The man's mouth opens, and his lower jaw drops to the floor.

"We'll get someone to clean that up for you." She taps her fingers against the desk. There is no computer. "Let me locate your reservation. One moment."

The man's loose arm falls off, tearing his shirt at the shoulder. Cly continues tapping her fingers on the desk, yellowed as old bone. It is bone, she realizes, hundreds of bones sanded together. It's no use, she won't be able to find the reservation. She doesn't have access.

"No matter," she says and heads toward the elevator, motioning for the guest to follow her. His one working leg drags his body after her. The door is made of slate. It opens onto a narrow, black cavern.

"In there," Cly says.

The man hobbles toward the edge. He looks back at her and for a moment, his face appears intact, recognizable, full of familiar sorrows. She gasps, just as he drops down into the abyss.

II

Exactly one week later, Edith returns. Guests aren't given a choice of desk, and their check-in and check-out times are assigned to them in advance of their visit. All the same, there she is, beaming in that sly, overconfident way, as if she knows a secret about her that Cly herself does not.

She takes a breath, begins her incantation. "Welcome . . ."

Edith cuts her off. "You didn't call." She purses her lips, shakes her head, scolding her with mock seriousness.

Cly doesn't know what to say. Edith is addressing her as herself, not the attendant. She fingers the gold tree around her neck. "I'm sorry."

Edith laughs. "Really? You are? You don't *sound* sorry."

When she doesn't respond, Edith goes on. "How will you make it up to me, then?"

Cly blinks. "Excuse me?"

"I'm a dissatisfied guest." Edith purses her lips again. "What will you do to compensate me?"

Cly stares. There is no such thing as a dissatisfied guest here. Agitated, panicked, irate, yes. But it is usually with themselves that the guests have a problem. No one has ever complained about her.

"How about you let me take you out to dinner after your shift?"

"My shift ends quite late."

" 'Quite?' It ends *quite* late? Well, it just so happens I'm quite a night owl." Edith smirks. "An insomniac, really. That's why I come here." She offers this excuse casually, discarding it like something dropped from her pocket. Cly recognizes the lie. No one comes here just to sleep. "So, I'm sure I'll be awake. How late are we talking?"

"One a.m."

Edith laughs again, and Cly winces. She looks past her, glances around the lobby, worried Duke will somehow hear the laughter from inside his office and come lumbering out in a sour mood he'll hide for Edith's sake, then scold Cly after she's gone, getting too close to her, his breath foul.

"One a.m.? That's supposed to scare me?" Edith slaps the desk. "Let's have steaks at one a.m. then. Or gnocchi. Or sushi. I dunno, this is New York, you can have whatever you want. You aren't a vegetarian, are you?"

Cly opens her mouth to answer, but Edith cuts her off again.

"You can tell me later. It'll be a surprise." She winks.

When her shift ends, Cly slowly changes her clothes next to her locker downstairs. Then she heads out through the staff exit. She's jittery, flushed. It hits her when she sees Edith waiting for her across the street with her hands in the pockets of her fine leather jacket that this is not a joke or a game. Her nervousness morphs into panic. She looks around, checking for other employees. She sees a guy in coveralls, smoking, staring down at his phone. His uniform is the wrong color, he can't be from the hotel. But what if? If she gets caught fraternizing with a guest, Duke will fire her and she'll be exiled from the hotel. For a moment, Cly thinks about just going home. She could rush toward the train, pretend she hasn't even seen Edith waiting. But she finds herself drawn across the street and runs through the lanes, racing the oncoming traffic.

"You made it," Edith says, grinning. Cly isn't sure if this is a joke about her jaywalking or a comment on the fact that she's shown up at all.

"I could get fired for this," she says harshly, without thinking.

Edith touches her shoulder. Another electric bolt. Cly jumps.

"But it'd be worth it, I promise. C'mon." Edith puts her arm around her.

"Where are we going?"

"I don't know. I guess we'll find out when we get there."

They wander from block to block, passing groups of young, already-drunk pleasure seekers in fashionable garb, the kids out past curfew, the tired nighttime workers, some of whom are still wearing their uniforms. They walk by two bums sharing beers, clinking their cans together. The night is crisp, invigorating. There is a sense of celebration in the air, like it's New Year's Eve. They walk on till they reach a quiet, residential street shrouded by trees, only occasional lights on inside the buildings they pass. They are halfway down the block when Edith stops abruptly.

"We're here," she says.

"Where?"

They descend a few steps to reach a black, lacquered door, illuminated by a hidden light.

"Is this someone's house?"

Edith laughs. She opens the door and pulls Cly inside. They're at the threshold of a restaurant with low ceilings, the room softly lit. Opposite the door is a brick fireplace, a few logs smoldering. The décor is simple, classic, full of dark wood covered with plum tablecloths. The diners murmur, laughing, bringing sparkling glasses of wine to their lips.

The hostess greets them, shows them to their table without a wait, though the restaurant appears full. Waiters in stiff white shirts and black aprons hurry about with their trays. Cly eyes plates of lamb and seafood. Suddenly she's ravenous.

"This place has great steaks. I'm really in the mood for that," Edith says as they take their seats. She pulls her chair up next to Cly's. "You eat steak?"

Cly drapes her napkin over her lap. "Yes. I eat all kinds of things."

"Oh good. So you're not a vegetarian."

"I never said I was."

Edith laughs, touches Cly's hand. Zing, another shock. She must be doing it on purpose.

Cly takes a deep breath. "My parents are both European," she goes on. "So I've had things Americans don't like very much."

"Like what?" Edith turns to her, head forward, her elbow on the table. She fits her chin in her palm.

"Like, octopus."

Edith waves her hand at that. "Octopuses? We love those in New York."

"Rabbit."

"Personally, I love rabbit."

"Aspic?"

Edith makes a face. "Okay, you got me. Where are your parents from?"

Cly suppresses a sigh. Now she regrets mentioning them. "My father was . . . is . . . Greek, and my mother, French."

Edith raises an eyebrow. "My parents are both boring white people from a boring white place called Wisconsin."

Cly is glad to change the subject. "Is that where you grew up?"

But Edith waves the question away. "Tell me what it's like working in that hotel?"

"What it's like?"

"Yeah. I mean, you must see a lot of weird stuff."

Cly thinks of the man who threw himself out a window, how parts of him remained miraculously untouched by the fall. The hotel is twenty stories high. She sees the blood thickening in his hair. The man in her dreams, dragging himself through the interminable lobby to reach her desk, his body falling to pieces as he grins at her in apology. He doesn't mean to bother her, to cause trouble for anyone. He's heartbroken, that's all.

"No, not really," she says. "I don't know what guests do in their rooms. You'd have to ask housekeeping." She doesn't mention the team or their discreet handling of periodic breakdowns.

"And you don't talk to housekeeping?"

"No. I don't really talk to anyone." It just slips out. Cly blushes. She stands solitary at her post, even on her breaks. The other Check-In girls are mostly students, pretty girls she catches sight of now and then. They buy street cart falafel on their breaks, wolf down greasy slices of pizza while Cly eats nothing, put off by the idea of infusing her uniform with food smells, or risking an oily stain. The other Check-In girls slip each other notes, sneak around their desks between arrivals as if Duke is their curmudgeonly principal and not their boss. When they leave—or get fired—Cly will pick up their shifts.

Occasionally, a man in a cleaning crew jumper hurries by Cly's desk with his head bowed, sheepish. He knows he should use the tunnels instead of crossing her lobby. She squeezes her eyes shut as he passes, blotting out the sight of him.

Now Cly's cheeks feel hot and she's twisting her napkin in her lap. Edith has reminded her again that this is an indiscretion; she shouldn't even be here. She's also asking her questions about the hotel with a certain focus and intensity, which suggests there's something she's trying to ferret out. Cly doesn't want to imagine what Edith does in her own room, what housekeeping finds when they clean it in the morning. There are guests who weep until they pass out, who refuse to leave, break things, stuff orchids down the drain and flood the bathrooms.

In her time at The Gold Persimmon, Cly has noticed a pattern: there are those who have high-powered, stressful jobs, which are often accompanied by equally stressful home lives. They are the ones who flirt with her casually, almost perfunctorily, without really looking at her, the ones who come to the hotel under the guise of relaxing in solitude. The rooms have phones, but no outside lines. The guests are unreachable, their privacy absolute. They may wail, scream, puke, or suck a pacifier and no one will ever know.

Then there are the guests who come to the hotel because something happened. Their grief is pointed as a knife. Cly doesn't see as many of those, at least not at her desk. The man who killed himself was one. Now she can't help but wonder into which category Edith fits. Based on the clothes she's wearing, that she carries no purse or bag of any sort, and is out for a late-night dinner with her Check-In girl, Cly is pretty sure she has the answer. But it isn't something she really wants to know, not yet.

She's relieved when the waiter approaches. He gives them the specials, takes their drink orders. Edith chooses wine for them both.

"What are you going to eat?"

Cly has not even glanced at the menu. She looks at it now, balking at the prices. "I don't know. Maybe the halibut."

"No, no. Get the lamb," Edith insists, as if she somehow knows that is what Cly really wants, that she's only hesitating because of the cost. "And I'll have a steak, bloody," she adds with a grin.

They eat slowly, savoring each bite, sipping the wines the waiter agrees pair well with their choices, as though deciding what to eat could change the course of your life. But maybe it could, Cly thinks. She hasn't had such a dinner in a long time. The room is warm, full of murmured conversation and rich laughter. The lights wink. Though they are full from the meal, Edith still insists they order dessert, a flourless dark chocolate lava cake dusted with raspberry sugar. It melts in their mouths. Cly feels heavy, everything is happening in slow motion; she's drunk on the food and wine, the wood smoke and white lights tiny as flowers.

"Tell me why you work there," Edith says softly, leaning in close, breathing into the crook of her neck.

"Why?" She might as well have asked why Cly exists. "Where do you work?"

"I'm a pediatrician," she says quickly, dismissing the question. "I mean, why there of all places, with all those sad-sack people coming in?"

Cly shakes her head. Her hair rustles against Edith's. The world outside the hotel is uncertain, frightening. "It's not like that. It's a beautiful place. I love it there."

"You do?"

"Let's not talk about it anymore."

Edith threads her fingers through Cly's, kisses her knuckles one by one.

"Come back to my room with me."

Cly sits up. "What?"

"We'll sneak in. It's late now, no one will be around. Just come to my room." She reaches under the table and grips Cly's thigh.

"I can't do that."

She lets go of her leg and leans away. "All right."

Edith pays for the meal without ceremony. Cly is too embarrassed by the cost to say thank you. When they reach the street, she turns on her suddenly, her face expressionless, eyes hooded and dark, and pushes Cly up against the exterior wall of the building. Edith kisses her hard, hands roaming over her body.

"Are you sure?" She bites Cly's neck. It hurts.

Cly is shaking. "Yes," she says, though she doesn't know what she is saying yes to anymore. Yes, she is sure? Or yes, she wants to go to the room?

Just then, Edith's cell phone rings. "Shit." She turns away to answer it. "Hello? Yes?" She hisses into the phone. "I told you, tomorrow. Yes, tomorrow." She turns back to Cly and rolls her eyes. "Okay, okay. See you then." She hangs up.

"Who was that?"

"My mother. C'mon," she grabs Cly's hand and pulls her in close for another kiss, pressing the hand to her chest. Then she heads back the way they came, pulling Cly along.

"I'll take you to the train."

Cly is both disappointed and relieved. When they reach the subway entrance, they pause to kiss again.

"Give me your number. I don't want to have to wait for you to call me."

"I don't have a cell phone."

"What? How can you not have a cell phone?"

"I live at my parents' place."

Edith hands over her phone and Cly enters her home number. "They're always there. They're always awake. If you call, they will want to know who you are, everything."

"Your parents sound like very vigilant ghosts."

"Yes." Cly nods. "Exactly."

"Can I call you at work?"

Cly shakes her head. "No personal calls."

"But how would they know? Besides, I'm a guest." Edith smiles. Her eyes shine in the streetlight. They look more silver than blue.

"I will call you. I swear."

Edith kisses her, pushing her tongue into Cly's mouth as she rubs her breasts, tweaks her nipples through her bra. "You'd better."

Cly rides the subway home in a daze. It is nearly four in the morning by the time she reaches her neighborhood, an hour when normally she'd be terrified to walk around alone, but the danger seems far away as she plods along, eyes on her feet. She can still feel Edith's hands on her, tastes her in her mouth, the wine and flesh she's eaten mixed with something sweet, unnamable, something that is just Edith. When she reaches the apartment, she slips through the dark into her bedroom and goes straight to her desk drawer, where she's stashed Edith's number. She studies the digits till she's memorized them.

Outside, movements in the dark: rummaging, a crinkle and a shuffle, followed by a cough. Her parents are awake, sitting in the living room, which adjoins the kitchen. They've heard her come in, of course. But they go on pretending they're tucked into bed and asleep, not sitting there in the dark, watching, listening to her every move. Cly lies down on the bed and sighs, deeply. She rubs her breasts, pinches her nipples through the bra the way Edith did. She wonders if she should tell her she's a virgin, then quickly decides against it. What does that mean, anyway, to be a virgin? It means she is untouched, and yet Edith has already touched her, slid her tongue into her mouth. Cly falls asleep in her clothes.

III

When Clytemnestra told her parents she was dropping out of college, her father teared up and left the room. Her mother shook her head, lit a cigarette.

If Claire had let him, Yorgos would've framed Cly's kindergarten drawings and covered the walls of their apartment with them. He would've tried to convince guests they were valuable abstracts, early works produced by famous artists. When she went through a short story-writing phase in middle school, he had them all printed and bound in a book. He was blind to her mediocrity.

Meanwhile, her mother examined closely the finger paintings and scribbles Clytemnestra brought home, squinting at the muddy blots of color and crooked lines.

"You should do whatever brings you joy," Claire said. "But don't try to be a painter. You don't have it in you."

At the time, Cly didn't understand the connection between her art class projects and her future as an adult. Now she can see what her mother was up to, how she wanted to spare her from disappointment. Becoming a poet didn't prove easy for Claire. Her life was fraught with failure and rejection.

"You could still marry someone with money," she said after Cly's announcement, exhaling a fog of smoke that enveloped them both for a moment. She looked her daughter over. "You're very beautiful. You must know this. That is a woman's talent. Your father," the hand holding her cigarette gestured toward the bedroom, "he doesn't understand."

Yet it was after Cly dropped out that her mother stopped publishing. She went from declining invitations to give lectures and readings to ignoring them all together, slowly burning all the bridges she'd spent thirty years constructing. It surprised Cly that her mother thought that much of her, that what she did had the power to affect Claire like that. She was moved, yet it also frightened her.

Meanwhile, Claire grew even thinner. She shrieked and shouted over ordinary things: Why had no one put the dishes away? Why was the bed unmade? How could the neighbors make curry again? Didn't they know she couldn't stand the smell? She cried often, wiping at her eyes with the heels of her palms, smearing her makeup.

Claire had gone through many funks, depressions, and extended "moods" before, but this one developed rapidly. It pulled her under. Every time Cly arrived home from a shift at the hotel, her mother seemed a little more shrunken, her lipstick less precise, her eyes sharper yet sitting deeper in her head, her teeth gray as dull, tiny knives.

One day, she was crying and wouldn't come out of her room. Cly called her father's cell phone several times, but there was no answer. He was always losing his phone, and even when he managed to hold onto it, he never seemed to hear it ringing or buzzing. It was an entirely foreign object to him, something he could not manage to associate with himself or his family. So she went to the university to fetch him, her stomach churning with nausea, acid working its way up her throat as she crossed the expansive lawn toward his office, a little room in the basement of one of the humanities buildings. It was fall, and the campus was all bright sun, gold and red leaves; the grass still impossibly verdant. As Clytemnestra approached, she saw Yorgos standing outside, talking to a girl. She stopped in her tracks. The girl had fine, blond hair and wore an oversized sweater and jeans, a backpack hanging from her narrow shoulders. That big sweater accentuated how tiny she was, how skinny and narrow-hipped, the kind of girl with long feet and fingers.

Cly observed the way they spoke, thinking they were alone: how they leaned in close, smiling into each other's mouths. The girl's shoulders were slightly hunched. Her father kept his feet apart. Then she loped away as Yorgos turned and trotted down the steps toward his basement office. Cly followed, pausing in front of the tall wooden door that had closed behind him so he wouldn't realize she'd seen him.

"Maman is ill," she said when she finally reached the office. She didn't say hello.

Yorgos stared at her in bewilderment for a moment. Cly knew it was because she was out of context; she didn't belong in his university world.

"All right. Yes," he said at last. He picked up his coat and slung it over his arm. "I'm coming."

He had always had his favorites and was a favorite in turn. He was still passionate, lectured wildly and unabashedly, learned most of his students' names and read many of their papers himself, instead of turning the work over to his TAs. He wrote tough yet detailed comments by hand, gripping his pen too hard. Once or twice, Cly sat in on his classes—"Tribal Violence in Ancient Greek Literature" was her favorite—and she could always tell which were the ambitious ones, the ones who wanted the respect and hard-won praise of a father figure, her father. She and her mother called them "The Audience." They lingered after class to ask carefully planned-out questions, sent him emails over the weekend that sometimes made him laugh out loud.

Yorgos swore he never touched the girl, and Clytemnestra believed him, not that it mattered. There was nothing sexual in the letters and emails. Instead, he confessed his doubts: about himself as an academic, as a husband, a father. He opened his heart to her and then, in the end, she showed it all to the dean. The school called their relationship "an unhealthy attachment." It was as if he had gathered all his hopes and pride in his daughter and neatly transferred them to someone else, like a piece of jewelry or furniture, something that could be given and taken away.

Did the girl actually care for her father at all? Clytemnestra often wonders. She remembers the student's posture, the humble curve of her spine, the way she looked at Yorgos's face, then down at the ground, or at a tree behind him. How could she have betrayed him? Or did he betray her somehow?

Her father's relationship with his student was a consequence of Cly's own failure. He wanted a daughter who was not just a student, but a scholar. And her mother, despite craving drama, wasn't strong enough to bear the weight of Yorgos's shame. Somehow, Clytemnestra managed to ruin both of her parents' lives. To end them, essentially.

If only she could've gone back. Transferred somewhere else—the city was full of colleges. But it didn't matter which school she chose and she knew it. The problem wasn't disinterested teachers or giant, musty lecture halls. Cozy seminars were not the solution either. The problem was something in Clytemnestra herself. She coasted well enough through high school, but then it was as if at graduation, a switch flipped inside her. As soon as she entered a classroom, she floated up out of her body. She watched the whole thing from the ceiling, studying the snowy patterns of her peers' dandruff. She watched them take notes. She could hear the teacher talking, along with the occasional responses from the students, but the sound was too big and slow, like words shouted underwater. It took all of her concentration to decipher even a portion of them. The effort lit the inside of her skull on fire and then she was helpless from the pain, good for nothing. All she could do was close her eyes. It got so bad that just setting foot on campus made her sick. No, Clytemnestra couldn't study. It was not a question of philosophy versus literature or economics. From the ceiling, she pulled at her hair and strands fell slowly like black spider's silk over the students. They didn't notice. No, she couldn't do it.

If she couldn't be a student, then she could work and contribute to the household. Any job would do.

Cly saw pictures of the hotel in the news: the modern, unassuming exterior. She was curious about it the way she would've been a new monument or museum exhibit. Then, she entered the place for the first time.

Duke told her which door to use, and to tell the desk she was there to interview. But the moment Cly crossed the threshold at Check-In C, wearing a blouse and a vintage pencil skirt that belonged to her mother, the stillness seized her, threw a quieting tarp over her mind. She held her breath. There was a girl at the desk, patiently absorbing the look of her. She directed Cly to the manager's office.

"You seem quiet. You'll do great," Duke said when he hired her.

She merely nodded in assent, proving his point. It was meant to be.

At The Gold Persimmon, she's required to whisper. To smile, but not too big or for too long, to conceal her teeth. To speak in hushed tones, look away from the hurt in a guest's eyes. Inside the hotel, her thinking is sharp. Everything there is quiet, pristine, no matter what happens outside, or what she might come home to.

Cly took her mother to one doctor, then another. They kept discharging her, not because they thought she was well and didn't need treatment. On the contrary, one doctor confided. She was young, a bit more tolerant than the others. Her short, brown hair hung in a slant across her forehead and she tossed her head every few seconds to keep it out of her eyes. Cly became mesmerized by that gesture. She pinched the collar of her jacket and tugged at it. Her mother would've teased her if she saw.

"I know that look." One eyebrow shot straight up her forehead. The opposite eye squinted. According to Claire, young, pretty lesbians were always in style. In middle age, they grew stout and dowdy. It was something to watch out for.

"Your mother will never be completely well," the doctor said. "In fact, I have concerns about what could happen if she doesn't start taking care of herself."

"The smoking?" Cly offered. "It's the smoking, right?"

The doctor looked at her pityingly. She put a hand on her arm and squeezed gently, the touch exuding heat Cly could sense through her sleeve. "She's a combative patient. I'm afraid I can't help her."

That was the end of that one, too. They went through three more before Claire decided she'd had enough. "No more appointments," she sneered at the word, as if it were equivalent to some horror—"gallows" or "internment camp."

Cly didn't argue with her. She believed what the young internist had told her, and she knew there were few decent doctors left in the city who would've taken her mother as a patient.

Yorgos, meanwhile, said nothing about any of this. He knew better than to get involved in such matters.

"I gave up telling your mother what to do years ago," he told Cly. It was late at night, after she'd come home from a shift at the hotel. Claire was asleep, the only time they could find to be alone together. Sometimes they had a brandy and whispered in the dark. "You should do the same."

"I will, Papa."

IV

Edith stays at the hotel once a week, always during one of Cly's night shifts. Each time, they go somewhere new for dinner, places Cly never would have imagined exist. They sit on the floor in a private room with a rice paper screen to eat sushi with their fingers, their waitress in a fine kimono, her hair done up in such elaborate loops, it must be a wig.

A small, navy box with a chrysanthemum-white bow on top materializes on the table. Edith grins at it. Slowly, Cly takes it apart. Inside is a tiny gold broach, shaped like a persimmon. She stares at it. It's real gold yet it feels cheap somehow coming from Edith and not the hotel, like a sacred symbol printed on a T-shirt or a hand towel.

"You like that? I was buying these earrings and I saw it." Edith tucks her hair behind her ear, revealing a tiny gold triangle affixed to the lobe.

Cly murmurs a thank you, puts the broach in her pocket.

Edith looks around the room. "Aren't the owners of your hotel Japanese?" She smirks. She always calls it "your hotel."

Cly doesn't know for sure; no one does.

"Mm, so many secrets," Edith mocks.

Cly is surprised she doesn't seem to know about The Accident. Sometimes people looking for ghost stories try to book rooms, but the one-adult-per-room occupancy rule, plus the policy against children of any age, usually deter them. She keeps planning to bring up the story with Edith, but something holds her back.

After each dinner, Edith makes an attempt to get Cly into her room. By now, their desire has reached a fever pitch. They kiss in doorways and under awnings, grinding their hips against each other like teenagers. Nevertheless, Cly declines.

"I can't lose my job," she says, though what she really means is she can't lose the hotel. They can't go to her apartment, either. Edith never invites her to her home and Cly is afraid to ask why.

And then, one night, they're having cocktails and eating pizza with lemon, ricotta, and artichoke hearts at a place with brick walls and spacious, red leather booths, succulents in little jelly jars on the tables made of polished driftwood, an antique jukebox in the back playing Sinatra, when Edith grins, tells her she has a surprise.

"A surprise?" Cly wipes her mouth with a paper napkin. She thinks of the broach, hopes it isn't another piece of jewelry.

Edith slides something across the table. She lifts her hand with a flourish to reveal a slim, gold cell phone.

Cly stares at it. The phone gleams, a plastic sticker still affixed to the screen. More gold. Cly would've chosen black.

"What's this?"

"It's a communication device. I don't know if you've heard of these? Might make it easier for me to reach you."

Cly shakes her head. "I can't accept this."

"Of course you can." Edith places the phone in her palm, closes her fingers around it. "It's yours." Her voice is soft yet firm. She kisses her hand and grins.

"Anyway, this isn't the surprise."

Cly looks up. The hand with the phone in it feels heavy. It sinks into her lap. "What do you mean?"

"You'll see."

After dinner, Edith takes her back the wrong way. "Tell me," Cly begs, but she refuses.

They stop in front of another hotel. Cly knows this one, as she knows all the competing hotels in the city. It's a run-of-the-mill establishment, opened in the twenties, stuffy and ostentatious.

"What are we doing here?"

Edith kisses her. "We have a room for tonight."

Cly tilts her head back to take in the building, its pompous flags waving. "Here?"

Edith grabs her hand, pulls her up the steps to the entrance. "C'mon."

As they check in, Cly scans the lobby. The floor is a mirror, casting shadows like blackbirds that swallow everyone's toes as they walk by. What if someone works at both hotels and catches her here? Even if they didn't tell Duke, the rumor of her infidelity would spread.

Edith leans in close, whispers into her hair, "You'll feel better once we get upstairs."

The room is a suite, almost the size of Cly's apartment. It looks like the inside of a dollhouse, the walls pastel, all the furniture Louis XV. Anything possible to upholster is covered in floral print. It's too much, but there's something regal about it, like being inside a painting: the basket of fruit on the coffee table dripping with pale grapes, vases of white and pink peonies crowning the vanity and nightstands. The bed is king sized, fluffy. Cly flops down on it and sighs.

"See?" Edith lies down next to her. "I told you you'd feel better."

But this isn't like their furtive make-out sessions in front of restaurants. There will be no surreptitious caresses under a table here. This is a real room with a bed and windows with drapes. It's the first time, Cly realizes, that they've really been alone.

Edith begins kissing her neck, slowly stroking her limbs. She runs her finger in a circle around Cly's palm. When Edith undoes a button on her blouse and Cly stiffens, she refastens it.

"We have all night," Edith says.

Cly thinks of her parents: a glint of eye in the dark, the chink of ice in the glass. She shuts her eyes.

Edith gets up and dims the light, then slowly takes off all her clothes. When she's naked, she climbs into bed. There's a series of pink, italicized stretch marks punctuating her abdomen.

"Come on, get in," Edith says.

Cly strips down to her underwear and joins her under the covers. She lands a hand softly on Edith's rib cage, then moves clumsily, too fast, hesitating to touch her stomach. Her body is taut, muscular, only the belly loose. Cly traces the stretch marks.

"Where did you get these?"

Edith stiffens. "Oh. I used to be kinda fat. I have them here, too. See?" She pulls back the sheets, rolls onto her side and shows Cly her hip. "And here, too." She pats her ass.

Cly nods. Now the mood has shifted. She pulls her lover in close, kisses her desperately, as if to erase the past few minutes. Edith responds eagerly, chuckling into Cly's mouth as she reaches around to unhook her bra.

"At last," she sighs when Cly is naked. The length of Edith's back is there, visible in the black mirror of TV behind her. There, too, are Cly's own hip and thigh, her breast. She watches the bodies wrestle till they consume each other.

*

Cly leaves the hotel in a daze. On the subway ride home, she keeps smelling her own hands, locks of her hair, everything infused with Edith's scent. She blows into the apartment.

"Where have you been?" An echo of Claire's voice, following her into her room.

The smell of cigarette smoke drifts in.

"It's about time you had a lover," she hears her mother say. "I'd already had five by the time I was your age."

Cly begins brushing her hair, then busies herself with fresh socks and underwear from her dresser. "I have to get to work, Maman."

Now her mother's face appears, disembodied, floating in the doorway. Her lipstick is crooked, a red scrawl. The eyes, narrowed, watch Cly move about the small room. She can't resist the opportunity to tell her again to quit her job, stop wasting her time working as a chambermaid. It's the song she cannot stop singing.

"That's not what I do," Clytemnestra says. She took a shower at the hotel with Edith, but she needs to change her clothes and she doesn't want to strip now, in her mother's presence.

"Can you give me some privacy?"

An overplucked eyebrow arches sharply. "Fine." The door slams.

But Cly can still hear her mother, as clearly as if she were speaking in her ear, complaining in rapid French to her father, her words sharp as pins pricking the bright balloons hanging above them, pop pop pop, as she recites her list of grievances against the neighbors, the building, the city itself. All the false poets, the sycophants she despises, otherwise known as her fans. She adds Cly to the list.

"And this daughter who acts like a teenager, coming and going as she pleases. Doesn't she know I need quiet? I need peace? This is why I can't work. This is why. You all suffocate me."

Now comes her father's murmuring that she can never make out. It doesn't matter, everything he says is wrong. On cue, Claire begins to wail. Though her shift doesn't start for another two hours, Cly hurries out of the apartment.

Outside, everything is peaceful, bathed in sunlight, the neighborhood quiet, cars rolling slowly up and down the avenue, honking half-heartedly, squirrels scrabbling after each other in the trees. This, she tells herself, out here, is real life.

That in there is not. She reaches into her pocket, pulls out the new cell phone, and calls the only number listed in her contacts, no name assigned to it.

"Missed me already?"

Cly smiles into the phone. "Yes. Where are you?"

"I'm at home. Actually . . ." she pauses. "I'm alone today. Wanna come over?"

Cly hesitates, considering this word, alone. "I have to work."

"Call in sick."

She's never missed a shift. "I can't."

Edith sighs. "You know, you complain about never seeing where I live. We can't go to your house. So I finally invite you over, and you decide work is more important."

"It's not just work." It's the precise mechanism of the hotel's routine, the comfort of fulfilling her role in the ritual. "I have obligations." But even as she says it, she already knows she's going to give in. "I don't even know where you live."

Edith's tone softens. "In Brooklyn, baby."

It turns out Edith lives in a brownstone in Park Slope. Cly can't remember the last time she was in that neighborhood, if ever. It takes her over an hour to get there. The neighborhood has the same air of residential quiet as her own, the same tree-lined streets. Except here there are thirty-something women in yoga pants pushing strollers instead of elderly men walking dogs.

Cly's shaking as she approaches the house and rings the bell. She bounces on her heels, thinks about the naïve co-eds who used to track Claire down and buzz at their door, usually girls who read her poetry in high school and identified with the anguish and rage. If Claire had ever had a conversation with them, Cly knew she would've explained exactly what they'd missed, how their suburban, corn-fed existence made it impossible for them to grasp her work.

Claire never let them in, though. She told the first few through the intercom to go write a fucking dissertation. Later on, as she grew quieter and retreated further into the recesses of her notebook, she began to ignore the buzzer altogether. For a time, Cly's father answered.

"No," Yorgos shouted wearily into the intercom, "there is no one here by that name." In a way it was true, he said, because none of his wife's devotees could correctly pronounce her last name, whether they tried the Greek or the French.

These days, the buzzer stays quiet.

Edith opens the door in bare feet. She's smiling. She hugs Cly right there at the threshold, then pulls her in.

The moment Cly steps inside, something feels wrong. She looks around, notes the den off the foyer, the oriental rugs and piles of books and shiny knickknacks. Down the hall on the right is the kitchen. She can see the tile from here, smells scorched toast and lemon cleaning spray. This can't be Edith's house.

"What is it?"

Cly shakes her head, forces a weak smile.

"C'mon." Edith grabs her by the wrist, pulls her into the kitchen. She sets about making tea. Cly stands on the opposite side of the island counter. She searches for something, though she's not sure what—a clue. There's a bowl of fruit, a neat pile of mail beside it. Adjoining the kitchen is a dining room with a dark-stained oval table, navy blue place mats at each setting. A white moth orchid sits in the middle. The pattern on the ceramic pot matches the place mats.

Slung over the back of one of the dining room chairs is a man's tie. Dull, navy blue, with fine red stripes.

"Hello?" Edith waves her hand in Cly's face.

"What?"

Edith stares at her. "I asked you what kind of tea you want."

"Anything is fine. Black. Black tea."

Edith gives her another look, then turns her back to her, opens a cabinet.

"You don't have work today?"

"I had a few appointments. I cancelled them. It was a slow day."

"What happens if you're not there?"

Edith shrugs, sets a sugar bowl and a jar of honey on the counter. "They see someone else."

"You don't worry they'll like that person better, that they won't come back?"

"Jesus, what kind of question is that?" Edith scowls. "They're kids. You think they'll leave me for another doctor?"

The kettle's hiss swells to a whistle. Edith turns off the stove, pours the hot water into two mugs. She slides Cly's cup across the counter toward her.

"I'm starting to regret inviting you over."

Cly startles, almost spills her tea. "But I took off work to be here."

Edith stirs in sugar, stares down into the mug. "Right. Time away from your precious hotel."

It is precious, Cly thinks. Lately, she's begun to wander on her breaks, just around the first two floors. She enjoys walking past the identical doors, not knowing who, if anyone, is inside. Sometimes she swears she can hear weeping and once, the mew of a cat. But she knows it's all in her head—no sounds escape those rooms.

"I won't get paid."

"I see." Edith's voice is flat. "I forgot there are people depending on you." She rolls her eyes.

Cly tries to speak, but her voice breaks. She turns away so Edith won't see she's tearing up. Edith leans over the counter, grabs her by the chin, and pulls her face close to her own. She shushes her, kisses her softly. Then suddenly Edith surrounds her, presses her face into her shoulder. She kisses her head, her cheeks, leads her back to the foyer, up the stairs. Several closed doors line the hallway on the second floor. The very last one Edith opens to reveal her bedroom, white curtains drawn, muting the sunlight. The bed is pale blue. Edith lays her down atop the duvet. Cly shuts her eyes, feels her lover's mouth, her body moving on top of her. She inhales deeply. The blankets smell of musk and wood, some kind of cologne mixed with skin and hair, unfamiliar oils. Cly opens her eyes, sits up.

"What is it?" Edith is panting beside her.

Cly stands, pulls her T-shirt over her bare chest. "Who else is living here?"

"What?"

"You said you were alone. Who else would be here, Edith?" She speaks quickly, without thinking, her voice high, and her lover's name comes out French, the accent slipping effortlessly into her speech. *Eh-deet.*

Edith leans back, propping herself up with her arms. "Would you like to meet him?" Her voice is controlled, quiet.

"Him? Who's him?"

Edith looks her hard in the eye as if to say, *Come on now, you silly girl.* "My husband."

Cly's stomach drops.

"I mean, you had to know. It's pretty obvious, don't you think?" Edith gestures toward the room around her.

Cly covers her mouth, swallows hard against a swell of nausea.

Edith stands up. "Don't be like that. Look, he knows, okay? He knows."

"You're married." Cly forces the words out, finally. *Of course*, she thinks. She imagines her mother's smirking red lips, crooked and garish, her cigarette stained from her kiss. "A proper affair," she'd say. Someone married, a woman, no less. And then certainly Claire would have her own story about an affair with a woman, an heiress, or maybe a dairy farmer's daughter. "Brava." She'd clap.

Cly gets up off the bed, then immediately sits down on the floor. "I think I'm going to be sick."

"Oh, come off it. Don't be so dramatic. It's not what you think. We have . . . an understanding."

Clytemnestra looks up at her. "He knows about me?"

"Well, in a general sense, yes."

"And now I know about him."

"Look, this isn't adultery," Edith says, rolling her eyes at the word. "There are parts of my life that are my own, just as he has parts of his life that are his own. We're very honest with each other, but this really has nothing to do with him. And he knows that."

Cly nods as if she understands.

"So conventional," her mother says, flipping through the pages of her notebook, her skinny legs drawn up like a schoolgirl. "So boring, my daughter." She shakes her head. "Tsk tsk."

"And what about Papa? That student wasn't even his lover."

Her mother slaps her notebook shut and glares.

"Would you feel better if you met him?" Edith sidles up next to Cly, lightly strokes her hair. "He would be fine with that."

Cly shakes her head violently. "I don't want to meet him." The tears race each other down her face.

Edith sighs and wraps an arm around Cly's shoulders. "I'm sorry, baby. See?" She chucks her under the chin. "Now we're ruining this whole perfect day. Think of all the things I could be doing to you right now." Grinning, she nips at Cly's neck.

"Do you and he, do you still . . ."

"What?" Edith feigns shock, her mouth an exaggerated 'O.' "Not that it's any of your business, but no, we don't still . . ." She smiles and encircles Cly's waist. "Actually, we never really did much to begin with," she mutters.

"This is weird."

Edith stiffens. "Yeah? Well, that's life, baby. Love is weird. It's all fucking weird. You can accept it, that it isn't all perfect like the fairytale erotica you got off to in high school, and just take the happiness you can get in whatever form it comes, or you can hold out for something that isn't weird, something that has no warts or bumps or whatever. But you'll be waiting a long time, babycakes. You'll be waiting forever." She sighs. "Look, I wanted certain things. I needed certain things." Her voice softens. "Maybe it's hard to understand at your age. I don't know if I really got it then. But you'll see, this is really the best way." She grabs Cly's face, pulls her in for a kiss.

Cly lets Edith kiss her, tells herself she's leaving, in just a minute she'll be out the door and back on the subway, heading toward a café, a museum, Central Park. Somewhere she can spend the day pleasantly alone. Soon, she is naked. Hours pass. They spend the day in bed, alternately fucking and eating and fighting. When they fight, Edith raises her voice, and Cly cries. The bed is full of crumbs, wet spots, black strands of Cly's hair.

When it starts to get dark, Edith tells her it's time to go. "He'll be home soon."

Cly realizes Edith hasn't named this husband. She's not sure she wants to know.

"Unless you wanna stay? Meet him, have dinner with us?"

In response, Cly throws on her shirt.

"Hey," Edith says, laughing. "I'm just kidding, all right?"

Cly nods. "I know."

When she leaves, Edith kisses her quickly at the threshold, then closes the door in a whoosh before Cly has even made it down the steps. From the sidewalk, she looks up at the house. It's like all the others on the block. The curtains are drawn now, the downstairs windows glow. Who knows what goes on in these houses? Who comes and goes, the lies that are told, the little deaths. *Les petites morts.* She looks around. The mothers with strollers have disappeared. Soon, all the husbands who were sent out into the world will return, bringing back fragments of it with them. She could stand there and wait until someone stops in front of Edith's house, opens the door with his own key. But seeing him would make him real.

She heads toward the subway.

That night, Cly dreams she's walking down a long hallway lined with identical doors. Behind one is her father, busy with work, happily composing lectures and papers for publication while her mother scribbles in her notebook in an adjacent suite, her wine half drunk, a cigarette burning down. They don't know Clytemnestra is there. She'll only find them like this if she opens the right door.

She makes her choice. The doorway opens onto an elevator shaft, bottomless, a gilded abyss. She stands at the edge, peering down into nothing.

V

The following week, Edith shows up at the hotel as usual and grins her way through check-in, tossing off little asides designed to throw Cly off her game. Cly smiles at her, indulging her the way she would any guest.

Still, when her shift ends, she hurries from the hotel toward Edith, casting worried glances over her shoulder. There's a guy in a uniform outside again, surely a different person, enjoying a quick break. She tucks her head, hunches her shoulders. He isn't watching, she tells herself. No one is watching.

When she arrives, Edith kisses her decorously, a peck, and they head back to the hidden restaurant where they first broke bread together. It's the only time they've gone back to the same place.

"I thought this might remind you why you fell for my charms to begin with, married lady though I may be." Edith bats her lashes.

Cly stiffens. She hates the way Edith jokes about her marriage. For two months, she made no mention of it at all; now she can't seem to stop.

"Hey," Edith puts an arm around her, "lighten up."

Inside, everything is just as Cly remembers, even the hostess, who seats them at the same table. The room smells like warm bread, lamb and steak with butter, herbs. Impossibly slim waiters zip by, all straight lines and right angles. Edith slides her chair over again, leaving no space between them. A cork pops and another table claps and cheers. This time, Cly orders a steak.

Their hands rest next to each other on the tabletop. Edith takes Cly's in hers.

"I'm glad you came out with me tonight."

Cly smiles politely, lays her napkin in her lap.

Edith squeezes her fingers, hard. "I mean it. I missed you."

She sighs, gently pulls her hand away.

"Okay, I know, I know. I deserve the silent treatment." Edith rolls her eyes, presses a hand to her forehead. "I've been bad. A very bad, wicked woman." She smiles.

Cly looks down at her lap, watches her fingers twisting her napkin into a rope.

"Haven't you ever wanted something so badly that you'd do anything to get it?"

She blinks. "No."

Edith sighs. "Well, that's a shame. I hope you will one day." She reaches for Cly's hand again, grips it firmly. "I want to be that thing."

"What thing?"

"The thing you'd do anything for."

"Risking my job isn't enough?"

Edith lets go of her hand. "Jesus, this again."

"What?" Cly checks to see if anyone is listening.

"Enough with the hotel, okay? It's just a shitty job. Stop acting like you're risking it all."

Cly sits up very straight, sucks in her lips. Her cheeks are burning.

Edith grabs for a piece of bread, tears off a chunk with her teeth. "You're wasting yourself there."

"I'm not."

"Really?" Edith bangs her hand against the table. Cly takes another furtive look about the room. No one so much as glances in their direction, they just keep on eating and talking. "What's so special about it then?"

It's my temple, Cly thinks. The quiet within your own mind: a sanctuary. Guests come from all over to purge themselves there. The gift is so great, it killed a man.

"You tell me. You're the one who stays there every week."

Edith's eyes go wide as she leans back in her chair. Then she cackles. "What a bitch you are!" She laughs loudly, pounds the table and the silverware jumps.

Cly sits there, stricken. Eventually, a waiter comes over, offers to refill their wine glasses.

"More wine!" Edith shouts. "Oh goodness, we need lots of wine."

The waiter demurs. "Very good." He disappears.

Edith turns her grin on Cly. "See, now we're getting to it. The ugly part. You say things to hurt me, I say things to hurt you."

"That isn't how this started."

"No, you're right. It started with me wanting to fuck you."

"Edith!"

"Don't you mean, *Eh-deet*?" She cackles again. The wine arrives. They wait as the server presents the bottle, then fills their glasses. Edith nods at him. When he's gone, she takes a big sip. "Just tell me one thing. Do you want to fuck me?"

Cly stares at her.

"Don't give me that shocked schoolgirl bullshit. Just tell me, do you want to fuck me?"

"Yes," Cly mutters.

"What? I can't hear you."

She blushes, head down. "Yes," she says again, this time a little louder.

"Hey," Edith lifts Cly's chin. "Look up. Look around. Nobody cares. You can scream it, they won't hear you. Now, do you like fucking me? Just nod. Okay, yes, you do? Good. That's all there is to it. We want each other, we like each other. We even . . ." Edith lifts one eyebrow, purses her lips. "Maybe we even something else each other. That's all that matters."

"But . . ."

"But what? You want me or you don't. It's that simple to me. If not, then you can just go. I'm not gonna play games with you. So if you're going to stay, you have to perk up, lose the attitude, and fucking kiss me like you mean it." Under the table, she forces Cly's thighs apart, touches her through her clothes. "Go ahead. That's it. Relax. No one cares. No one's watching."

Cly leans back, closes her eyes for a moment, then jerks upright and looks around the room again.

"I told you, no one's watching. No one cares. We can do anything we want. We're free." She kisses Cly's neck, begins to unbutton her pants.

"Wait, wait." Cly is breathing hard. She reaches for her glass of wine, gulps down a quarter of it.

"That's the spirit! Oh, I made a pun." Edith chuckles at her own joke. Her entire hand has worked its way into Cly's pants. "Just close your eyes, baby. And then there will be a big steak waiting for you."

*

After dinner, Cly half expects Edith to invite her to another hotel, but instead she announces she's heading back to The Gold Persimmon. This time, she doesn't try to persuade Cly to go with her. Instead, she pecks her on the cheek and takes off. Cly watches her go. She feels like Edith has something of hers, something essential as a house key, only she can't think of what it is.

When she gets home, there's a shadow by the window: a darker patch of deeper black, her parents standing in it, their backs to her, postures erect. In the bathroom, she thickens the air with steam. Half submerged in the tub, Cly wonders if that dinner tonight was even real, if she even did the things she thinks she did. In the pocket of her pants, lying crumpled on the floor, is the cell phone Edith gave her. If it was real, she decides, then Edith will call her tonight, even if it's just to say goodnight. In an instant she changes her mind. No, if Edith doesn't call, that means it was real.

The drain chokes on the bathwater. Her twin waits in the mirror, watches as she emerges. Teeth against the glass, dull yet pointed. Cly exhales, her head rears back. Edith is there in the doorway behind her. She mutters things too quietly for Cly to hear. One arm braces against the mirror, a hand covers her eyes. It could be Edith's hand, the scent of her fingers.

Cly finishes and lifts her head, eyes opening slowly. The first thing she sees in the glass is the open doorway. She spins around. There's no one there, yet she's certain the door was closed. She always closes the door. Shame breaks out across her face like a rash. She gathers up her clothes, ties her robe too tightly and rushes, chin down, to her room.

Just as she's getting into bed, the cell phone rings. They talk for a few minutes. When they're about to hang up, Edith lets out an "I love you," so nonchalant, as if she's said this a hundred times before. Is it just habit, a way to end a conversation? Cly lies there, staring at the little phone in her palm like it has all the answers to the questions she doesn't even know how to ask.

*

At first, Edith only books the most expensive hotels, the kind with rooms that look like life-size doll houses. More suites, more fruit baskets, more floral prints and antiquated furniture, the scent of old perfume, lilies and poppies—death flowers, vases of them, as if they are in town for the funeral of some old New York grande dame.

Then, bit by bit, the suites contract to the size of a single room. A bed, a heavy wooden desk, everything ornate, stuffy.

Next they move on to lesser hotels with more modern rooms, thin, cream-colored duvets, a smaller TV, beige walls, ugly geometric carpet, no flower prints. Cly prefers the simpler ones, though she doesn't say so. Edith says nothing at all to explain the downgrade yet she's offended by the change, complains about the room service menus, how they don't have anything she wants, though she orders something anyway. She bemoans the bathroom's lack of a luxurious tub. She scowls at the attendants, points out to Cly the stains on their pants, accuses them of needing haircuts. The Gold Persimmon has strict requirements regarding hair length, accessories, makeup. When employees come aboard, they must sign a contract, vowing to uphold the hotel's standards. It's the last test you have to pass. But Cly doesn't bother explaining this.

"Sorry to make you spend more time in a hotel." Edith rolls her eyes at their room, which has been declared too small, the view not to her liking, though they will be there for only one night and there's nothing out there to see, anyway, except lights and cabs cruising by. Cly notes this is the only time Edith has ever said "sorry" to her.

Every hotel lobby they enter is a train station with a dull, mechanical roar in the background, various squeaks and twitters rising above the din to make the blood throb in her temples like someone running up and down a flight of stairs. The check-in desk may be unmanned or worse, swarmed with employees, all chatting with each other, the guests squawking, making a racket.

The Gold Persimmon is a hotel in name only. The rest out there are just rooms to sleep in. Edith somehow still does not understand the difference, even though she spends one night a week there.

Now the steaks arrive, overcooked, of course. Edith persists in ordering things she knows she will be dissatisfied with, just as every mattress is either too hard or too soft for her liking.

"You have to lose your mind to find it again," Yorgos used to say. It makes Cly think of The Gold Persimmon's guests. How many people are truly alone? With no one at all who cares for them, no one who depends on their work, their money? Loneliness is not a lack of people and things to occupy one's life; it's a lack of connection with those things. The Gold Persimmon strips that away, too.

She tries to get Edith to forget about the steaks, tells her they should go out instead. But Edith's mood is spoiled. Now she's not hungry, she says. She sits on the bed, turns on the TV, and sulks. After a while, she pulls a few tiny bottles out of the minibar. Cly says nothing. Her stomach rumbles. Edith doesn't glance at her once, just keeps her eyes fixed on the TV, her hand ferrying the little bottle to her lips. She's watching a reality show about mythical woodland monsters.

"It could be here, in these woods," the host says, gesturing toward the trees.

Cly eats the cold steak. She falls asleep sitting up in a chair, leaving Edith in the bed. In the middle of the night, she wakes to find her clothes coming off.

"C'mon," Edith whispers, pulling her toward the bed. Her skin is blue in the electric glow of the TV. Cly allows herself to be stripped, maneuvered onto the mattress, made love to. She keeps her eyes closed.

VI

Edith leaves messages on Cly's phone, inviting her to her house again. Just the thought of that brownstone full of throw rugs and matching dishes—married-people things, so uncharacteristic of her lover—fills her with unease, as if she's already there, waiting until it's safe to leave.

But Edith insists. She's had enough. "I hate those hotels," she hisses into the phone.

Cly is on her lunch break, though she has no lunch to speak of. Instead, for the first time she goes outside to call Edith, so nervous to step out, she forgets her jacket and shivers in her thin blouse.

She imagines what will happen if she says no, forces Edith back into a rented room. She'll have to coax her out to have dinner, or else they'll end up with room service again. They may or may not have sex.

In the end, she caves, just as they both knew she would. But on one condition: she won't sleep in Edith's marital bed.

"Fine, we'll do it on the floor."

"I can't be in his sheets, I can't have sex with you in your bed."

"We don't sleep in the same bed," Edith insists. But Cly remembers the smell of the bed linens. She pictures the upstairs hallway, all those unopened doors. Behind one of them, at least, there must be a guest bedroom.

"Just not that bed," she says, and finally Edith agrees, sighing, as if it's really some kind of compromise and she hasn't already gotten her way.

After her day shift ends, Cly changes her clothes and heads to Brooklyn. This time, there's no one on the street. She imagines Edith clearing the whole neighborhood for her.

Tonight, she answers the door with a glass of white wine in her hand, jazz music spilling out of the house into the open air.

"Hi!" She kisses Cly on each cheek, then a peck on the lips, like she's an old friend coming for dinner. "I'm cooking!" she crows and gestures with her free hand for Cly to drop her things on the stairs. Then Edith brings her into the kitchen, which smells like potatoes, lemon, and rosemary.

Edith peeks into the oven. "I'm making salmon. You like salmon, don't you?" Before Cly can answer, she goes to the fridge and pulls out a bottle of chardonnay. "Here, have some wine." She fills a glass already set on the counter. Cly's mentioned to Edith a few times that she doesn't really like chardonnay, but she takes the wine all the same.

Beside her glass is a small, navy blue velvet jewelry box, crowned with a white bow. Cly groans inwardly. Another gift.

"Go on, open it." Edith smiles.

"Can I open it later?"

She shrugs. Scowling, she turns away.

Cly looks around the kitchen, noting that all the books, papers, ties, shoes, and other miscellany have been gathered up and hidden away somewhere. There are no pictures out, no greeting cards on the counter, not even a magnet on the fridge. The house has been stripped of any outward signs of the marriage it contains but it's there all the same, like an underlying scent, embedded in the wood, the carpets, musky and fungal, something Edith is probably so used to breathing in, she doesn't even notice it anymore. To Cly, it's so palpable, it makes Edith's efforts to sweep away all these objects seem even more obvious, and sad.

Now she doesn't know what to say, or what to do with herself. She keeps drinking the wine, even though all she really wants is a glass of water. Meanwhile, Edith busies herself with this and that, mixing a marinade, peering into the oven and squinting against the heat. She's wearing an apron. It's a simple white chef's apron, but an apron all the same, with a designer tag hanging off the hem.

"How were your patients today?" She can't think of anything else to ask.

Edith shuts the oven door for the umpteenth time and sighs. She reaches for her wine. "I'm actually taking a little sabbatical right now."

She turns away and begins washing the lettuce in the sink. "It's very intense, you know. I don't know if you can imagine." Edith sets the greens in a plastic spinner and starts scrubbing tomatoes with what looks like a nailbrush. "Anyway, a sabbatical will give me time for research."

Cly wonders whose idea this sabbatical was. "I wasn't aware you conducted research."

Edith shoots her a look. "Of course I do. I started out a researcher."

Cly is sure she's never mentioned this before but mumbles an apology anyway and starts turning the lettuce in the salad spinner, then pats down the tomatoes with a dishtowel when Edith is finished with them. A hotel is starting to seem like a better and better idea. Cly decides to see how dinner goes. After that, she can either propose they relocate, or just go home. Deep down, though, she knows none of those things will happen, that she won't even mention such alternatives. "It's not worth a scene," Yorgos used to say when they were out in public and Claire happened to be in a mood, determined nothing could please her, and Cly tugged on her father's sleeve, begging him to take them all home. Once, her mother threw bonbons at a waiter, hitting him square in the back. She cheered with each bull's eye. "Writers are eccentric people," Yorgos would say, "meaning they're all a little crazy."

But Edith is not a writer. She isn't an artist of any kind.

Now she wants to set the table. "Go get some napkins from the linen closet."

When Cly says she doesn't know where the linen closet is, Edith sighs.

"Upstairs," she points to the hallway, "the door opposite the stairs."

Without a word, Cly heads up to the second floor. All the doors look the same, and none of them are situated directly opposite the staircase. She studies her options, finally choosing one at the end of the hall. She knows before she opens it that it isn't the right one.

It's not a closet at all but a room, the shades drawn. Cly hesitates, then turns on the light, and there before her is a bedroom from a child's dream: pale pink carpet with matching pink and white polka dot wallpaper, even the little bed frame painted a light rose, with a frilly cover. There's a painted bookshelf, stenciled with more roses, and a miniature desk to match with a tiny, three-legged stool. When Cly steps in to examine the bookcase, she leaves fingerprints in the dust. At her feet is a little rocking horse with a pink mane, a name painted on it in a dark blush: *Alice.* A glint of something half-under the bed catches her eye. It's a gift, wrapped in shining peach paper. She bends over, spots a mass of them under the bed, dotted with an assortment of candy pink bows.

Cly backs out of the room, softly shuts the door. The next one she opens is full of shelves lined with towels and blankets, place mats and napkins at the bottom in an array of colors. She selects two periwinkle napkins, then heads downstairs.

When Edith sees which napkins she picked, she makes a face and sends Cly back to get navy blue ones instead. Without a word, she complies. This time, she doesn't look at the door as she passes by. When Edith serves dinner, she forces herself to eat, pretends to listen to her conversation. Afterwards, Edith's mood improves. She tells Cly she wants to have their coffee in the living room, then pushes her onto the couch and straddles her. Cly's body feels limp, pliable. She watches herself having sex with her girlfriend, their clothes on the floor, cushions pushed out of place.

Outside, night is descending on the neighborhood.

When they're finished, Edith takes all the cushions off the couch, revealing a pullout bed underneath, already made up with sheets. The sheets are periwinkle, like the rejected napkins. The blinds are drawn. Edith goes upstairs to change, leaves Cly in the living room to do the same.

She takes her clothes to the bathroom, locks the door, then perches atop the toilet with her yoga pants and T-shirt in her lap. She studies the wall. Periwinkle again. A framed print hangs there, a drawing of a little girl holding a bouquet of wild flowers. Cly studies the little girl's face, searching for traces of Edith, though the drawing looks old. Then she realizes it's just a generic child, culled from an artist's lackluster imagination.

It's too early to go to bed. All the same, Edith turns out the light and they climb under the covers, lie side by side without touching. Cly wonders if this is how Edith sleeps with her husband. There's still music playing somewhere, a lone saxophone's note floating, desultory, into the room.

Edith wraps her arms around her, throws a leg over her hip and pulls her in close, her body too hot, crushing her. She moans softly. Cly doesn't move. She is waiting, though for what exactly she doesn't know. Edith touches her and Cly shuts her eyes against the pink squiggles on her lover's stomach, just below the navel.

Cly has tried to retrace their steps, to visit in the daytime the places Edith takes her at night, but she can't ever find them; they're not there. In the daylight, she discovers only ordinary storefronts. The white lights illuminating the awning are gone, along with the sophisticated patrons, lost in their mirthful conversations, forever laughing, drinking their wine. She might as well smoke cigarettes. Then she thinks of The Gold Persimmon. There are two types of guests.

Edith sits up. "What is it with you?"

Cly doesn't know what to say, so she doesn't say anything at all.

"I can feel you drifting. You're not here."

How should she reply? *I opened the wrong door and wandered into the place you go in your mind to mourn. I walked into your memory. I'm never coming here again.*

"What?"

Cly realizes she's said the last bit out loud. "I can't come here anymore."

Edith sighs, throws up her hands. "We're not in the bed. Isn't this better than a hotel? What more do you want?"

"There's something here, a pall over the house. I can't explain it. It's like an allergen," Cly speaks quickly, as if her lover can't hear her that way. "I felt it when I walked in."

Edith goes quiet. Finally, she says, "You know, don't you?" She begins to cry fat, sopping tears. Suddenly it's pouring outside, the water beating against the windows. The trees sag. Edith buries her face in Cly's breast. She opens her mouth wide, searching, sucking, the wails unbelievably loud. Cly doesn't know what to do. She wants to go home, despite the look her mother will give her when she walks in. Instead, she puts an arm about the woman who has replaced her lover, the way you would a stranger who's suffered some immediate and fantastic loss. Edith convulses hard enough to snap a rib. Outside, the rain beats the pavement till the water floods the storm drains and washes over the street.

Somehow, they fall asleep. In the morning, the house is full of light, as if the storm never happened, dust motes suspended mid-air like tiny, electrified angels. Coffee is brewing and Edith's husband is there, waiting to fill his cup.

From her place on the pullout bed, Cly can see into the kitchen where the man stands leaning over the counter, fingers tapping expectantly. The coffee maker burbles, clicks as the pot begins to fill up. He wears a burgundy pullover; the back of his head is silver, the hair still thick. A black watchband on his wrist. That's all she can see. She searches for her clothes but they're not in the room. Neither is Edith. She's in the kitchen, talking to the man in a low, familiar tone.

Cly throws on an oversized T-shirt, then slowly raises herself off the bed, but the pullout squeaks anyway. She freezes, listening. The murmuring in the kitchen goes on. Now to find her clothes. She tiptoes into the foyer, recalling her bag and coat left on the stairs. Both are gone.

"Cly?" Edith calls from the kitchen, "Is that you? We're in here."

Cly enters the kitchen braless, her arms crossed over her chest. She's not wearing pants and her hair is mussed.

"So there she is," says the man, leaning against the counter, sipping coffee from a mug. He smiles brightly. His eyes are too wide, too much of the white showing, like a vintage cartoon. He holds out a hand for her to shake and Cly hesitates before she accepts it. His skin is dry, cool. There's a dusting of dandruff on his shoulder.

Edith's dressed, smiling, her hair combed. "Cly, this is Sven."

"Well, hello." He raises his mug, saluting her. His teeth are uneven and stained. "I've been wanting to meet you for some time now, but Edith always comes up with some excuse."

Edith rolls her eyes, thumps Sven on the arm. "That's not true and you know it," she teases. She offers tea, some breakfast. Cly declines.

"So," Sven clears his throat, "you work at that opulent hotel Edith goes to, the Gold Pomegranate?"

"Persimmon," Edith corrects him. She's at the sink, washing out the now-empty coffee pot. Her movements are slow, easy.

"And what do you do there?"

Edith turns, rolls her eyes again. "Oh God, Sven, really? That's what you want to ask her?"

"What? I can't ask her about her work? I'm just curious about this lovely young woman. A man comes home, finds a beautiful lady in his house, he can't ask some questions about her life?" He smiles at Cly, winks. "Tell me then, where you live, where you grew up, if questions about work are off-limits." His eyebrows wriggle. They are thick, unkempt, the same silver as his hair.

"I live in the city. I grew up there."

Sven nods and his eyebrows rise, asking for more. "And what drew you to work at the Gold . . . Persimmon?"

"Jesus, Sven, will you stop with that?"

"What?" He turns to his wife, still smiling.

"Don't you think everyone she meets asks her that?"

"Sure, because it's a fascinating place! There isn't another one like it. Nor one as expensive!" He forces a laugh and Edith glares at him. "You probably asked her that, too, when you met her."

Edith plunks down a glass of water and Cly chugs it, half choking. "I think I should be going." She coughs.

"No, no, no, you can't leave yet!" Sven sets down his mug, maneuvers around the counter to get closer to her, drops a hand on her shoulder. He smells of Edith's sheets. Cly goes rigid, tries to make herself smaller. "I just got to meet you. Can't you stay? All right." He lets his arm fall away, then holds up both hands, palms exposed, supplicating. "I know, I know. Let's address the elephant in the room, shall we?"

"Sven . . ." Edith warns.

"This is what I do. I'm a psychiatrist," he tells Cly, nodding at her, as if this explains everything. "I don't know if Edith told you that. No? Okay, you're in your lover's house. Her husband is here now, me." He puts a hand over his heart. "Certainly an awkward scenario in most cases, but Edith and I aren't like most people. And she cares about you, so I care. I'm a curious man." He smiles again.

Cly senses the hallway there behind her, the fresh air flowing in from under the door, traveling through the house around her. She wants to turn and run, leave her clothes and shoes and subway pass behind. Instead, she stands there, nodding at Sven, doing her best to avoid his eyes. His eyes are alien. She is afraid that she will throw up now, make a mess of their clean floor, the countertop. She imagines Sven standing beside her, frowning down at the pool of vomit. Maybe then he'd let her go.

Cly realizes he's waiting for her to say something. Meanwhile Edith's finished with her chores. She stands a few feet away, holding her own mug of coffee. Cly tries to send a distress signal but when Edith meets her gaze, she smiles blandly, eyes blank, as if they aren't much more than strangers.

Sven clears his throat again. "So, you live in the city. And you grew up there? Which part?"

Cly breathes fast through her mouth. She doesn't want to tell him where she lives.

"The Lower East Side." Now Edith catches her eye, a glimmer of recognition, the lie acknowledged but left unexposed. For now.

Sven begins sharing his opinions of the Lower East Side, how it's changed over the years, all the junkies and bars that used to be there. "Must've been very different when you were little," he says. Then he begins the story of how he came to buy this brownstone. The neighborhood was rough back then, the real estate value nothing compared to what it is now.

"Now, there's no way we could buy here, even with two doctors." He smiles, laughs again.

"Edith's on sabbatical." Cly blurts out. The words hang there in the air for a moment, all three of them staring, mouths tight, disbelieving.

Sven recovers first. "She told you about that?" He turns to Edith. "You told her about that?"

Edith shrugs. "I may have mentioned it."

"I see." Sven bobs his head. He smiles. His teeth are crowded together. The skin on his neck is loose and spotted. He's old. He is far too old, her father's age. She's sweating. They've been in bed together, the sheets smell of him. Together, they made a child. Cly sees his hips, his naked, sagging ass jerking between

Edith's legs. She tugs at her eyelashes, fights the urge to uproot them all.

Sven clears his throat again. "Edith is taking some time. The trips to the hotel were a kind of . . . experimental therapy we came up with, but progress is slow."

"Therapy?"

"Sven," Edith swats him with a dishtowel. "What the fuck are you talking about?"

He turns to her, mouth open, airing his teeth. "What? I thought you girls share everything." His voice has turned sharp, the smile savage.

"Come on, don't start this now. At least wait till she leaves."

Cly stands there threading her fingers through her hair, pulling out the loose, tangled strands. They drop to the floor.

"Will you look at her? Look at what she's doing." Sven points at Cly. "You're making her nervous, dear. Can't you see that? She's your guest and she's pulling her hair out."

Edith's laugh turns shrill as a birdcall. Cly's never heard her make that sound before. She slips her hands out of her hair and crosses her arms, covering her breasts again.

"Oh please. You're here all of a sudden when I told you to come home later . . ."

"You said, 'in the morning.'" Sven's fingers curl in the air. "You didn't say what time. If you wanted me to be here later, you should've said so. How was I supposed to know?"

"And you ask her about the hotel?"

"There's no shame in therapy. I'm a psychiatrist. It's my business. She knows." He turns to Cly, smiling aggressively, nodding, encouraging her. "She works there. It's not like she doesn't know people go there to grieve."

"Not everyone is there to grieve," Edith hisses, teeth clenched. "Jesus. Just shut the fuck up, dear."

Sven slurps his coffee, peering down into the cup.

Very quietly, Cly asks for her clothes.

"See," Edith erupts, "now she's leaving."

"Oh, let her go." Sven waves his hand. He lifts his head, beams at Cly. "It was so nice meeting you, dear. I hope you'll come back, maybe when Edith is in a better mood. You know how she gets." He winks.

Cly's stomach heaves. She clamps her jaw shut.

Edith opens a random cabinet, bangs it closed. "Your stuff is in the upstairs hall."

Cly rushes out of the room. There's her bag, sitting in front of the closet door, her clothes folded, piled on top. She turns her back to Alice's room, strips right there and throws on her street clothes, stuffing her yoga pants and T-shirt in her bag. When she lifts it up, she finds her shoes underneath and slides into them sockless.

Cly heads down the stairs. She's almost at the front door. "Bye," she calls over her shoulder.

Edith runs after her, grabs her arm. Cly grips the doorknob.

"Wait, I'm sorry. He wasn't supposed to be here."

Cly nods, hand still on the knob.

"I'll call you." Edith kisses her cheek, then disappears back into the house.

Cly pulls the door open, races down the steps, then doubles over and retches in a violent rush onto the sidewalk, the water she drank streaming out of her. She wipes her mouth when she's done, looks around. Is anyone watching? She glances at the house. The curtains are still drawn. Cly flees to the train.

When she gets home, she finds her mother perched sideways at the kitchen table, her skinny legs clad in tight black slacks slung over the arm of the chair, white feet floating, red toes bobbing, as if she's too thin for gravity to hold down. She smiles at her daughter.

Still wearing her backpack, Cly sits and drops her head onto the table with a thunk.

"I told you." Claire shakes her head.

"Told me what? You didn't tell me anything."

"I told you." Claire nods. She lights a cigarette.

"Let me have one."

Claire holds out the pack and Cly selects a cigarette, long and thin, the paper bright white. It feels good between her fingers. She inhales, then coughs furiously. It's stale.

Claire smiles. Her teeth are stained. On top of that, a little lipstick has rubbed off. "I told you."

Cly takes her cigarette to her room and lies on the bed. She holds it out to one side between her two fingers, lets the smoke drift in a thin strand toward the ceiling. She doesn't care about the smell now. She imagines tossing the cigarette right into the little black pit of Edith's mouth, the way it would sizzle as it disappeared down her throat.

When Edith calls that night, Cly doesn't pick up. Claire appears, a shadow in the doorway, watches her daughter cover her face with a pillow. The phone goes on ringing.

"Are you going to answer?"

She shakes her head and the pillow rustles. "It's too much."

"Yes, my love. It is always too much."

Cly sits up, pulls the pillow off her face. Her mother—the artist, the keen observer of the world—has disappeared into the recesses of the apartment.

When Cly was twelve, Claire published a book of poems about motherhood. She'd been accumulating them since Cly's infancy. The poems were fine-pointed tools, jabbing at the reader, prickling the heart, yet they were elusive, hard to grasp, like all her mother's work. Though she could not really understand the lines, Cly still felt their bitterness and loss. At her mother's readings, the audience members spoke to Cly carefully, sometimes with pitying smiles. She could tell they wanted to know how much she understood of her mother's poetry. But Cly didn't care what they thought. She liked watching Claire at the podium, the way everyone fell silent when she spoke, the nasal rumble and roll of that voice. She liked the way she laughed when it was all over, taking in the applause, then walked around holding a cup of ruby wine in her long, slender fingers. She gave Cly sips from her cup and introduced her to fellow poets and academics who smiled when they couldn't quite make out her name wrapped in her mother's accent.

"Cly—Sorry, what is your name?" they said, hunched over so their faces were close to hers. Her parents started calling her "Cly" as a joke but it carried on into adulthood. She could be Clytemnestra in private—unpronounceable, foreign, beautiful—and simply Cly in the world.

"Clytemnestra," her mother repeated, curling her lip, eyes rolling. Then she walked away and spoke to someone else, as if to say that was all the patience she had for that person who couldn't pronounce her daughter's name. Cly followed her. They held hands, even though she was too old for that.

Meanwhile, her father was off in a corner, oblivious to all but the intense debate he was having with one friend or another. Yorgos could never speak to more than one person in an evening and Claire teased him about it, how he left her all alone at departmental gatherings and dinner parties. It was a great joke because all three of them knew Claire didn't need anyone's help, she didn't care what other people thought.

But she grew pensive on the ride home. They were in a taxi, Claire wrapped in furs, Cly nestled against her. Her father was hunched over, asleep in the front seat beside the driver.

"They will hate your success," she told her daughter. She pulled her in closer.

Cly nodded in the dark. Everything her mother said was always true.

"So they will smile to hide their jealousy. People are only truly nice when they pity you," Claire whispered.

Cly thought of the adults, listening to those poems, stealing glances at her. Already, she knew what her mother meant.

They arrived at the apartment, Yorgos groggy, stumbling after them up the stairs. A little while later, Cly heard her mother crying in her bedroom. She listened through the walls to the warm muffle of her father's voice.

Her mother disposed unceremoniously of the mice that broke their necks in the traps set in their kitchen. She argued with Cly's most formidable teachers, cut fierce old ladies in line at the Jewish-but-not-kosher deli and the neighborhood pharmacy, then glared, daring them to confront her. When Cly attended her first and only sleepover, a ritual she was only invited to participate in because the girl's mother forced her to include everyone in the class, she brought a collection of Greek myths with her, a gift from her father, with an inscription inside the cover. The others doused it in ketchup and threw it in the trash. When Claire came to collect her and heard what had happened, she told the girl's mother it was people like her who were responsible for the Holocaust. Yet she cried the same way Cly did, with squeaks and moans. What could make her mother do that? Cly wanted to cry herself, with her mother's arms wrapped around her. She always wanted her most when she knew she couldn't have her.

VII

After a week of declining Edith's calls, the moment Cly's been dreading arrives, the one where her lover breaks the stillness and shoves open the lobby doors, then glares at the empty room, furious for her lack of an audience. She casts accusing looks at the furnishings as she stomps her way up to the desk.

"What the fuck?" she shouts, and Cly sucks in her breath, instinctively sets her palms over the desk as if to hold it steady.

"Please keep your voice down."

"Are you serious? You ignore me for a week and then you tell me to keep my voice down?"

Something sharp is jabbing at the interior of Cly's eye. She shuts it for a moment, tries to rub out the pain, but it's deep, she can't reach it. "Let's just get through this."

Edith rears back, starts to roar. "*This? What is this?*" She slaps the desk with the flat of her palm.

Cly leans back, looks down at her own hand, inches from the phone. She could call Duke, report a combative guest. The team would come. She's seen them only once. They look like hospital orderlies, all in white. Once they file up to a guest's room, that's that, she never sees the guest again. But then Edith would tell Duke everything. She doesn't care if Cly loses her place. The thought makes her throat tighten.

"There is an expression," her mother interjects, "about shitting and eating." Claire waves her hand, dismissing the thought. "I can't remember it now, but it applies to you."

While Edith rants on, Cly sets about checking her in, hoping to move her out of the lobby and into her silent room as soon as possible. Her lips are set in a line, her brow furrowed as her fingers rush nimbly over the keyboard's tiles. She is angry. Not at Edith, but at herself.

"Are you even listening to me?"

Cly looks up from the screen. Edith's eyes are wet, wide, her mouth hanging open. Now she notices what she missed before: the dark circles under the eyes, her unwashed hair, the leather jacket gone, replaced by an old sweatshirt Cly knows Edith wouldn't be caught dead in outside her house.

"Cly?" she dissolves into tears. Her hand grips her own neck as she sobs wildly, head tilted back.

Cly slides the key card across the desk. "Here."

Edith wipes at her nose, sniffs. "Are you coming with me?"

She shakes her head. "You know I can't."

"Enough with the fucking rules. This really isn't worth it to you?"

Cly takes a deep breath. "I can't come now. I'll come later."

Edith draws closer to the desk. "When?"

"Tonight. When I get off."

Edith smirks at the accidental pun and Cly blushes, embarrassed for her childish lover, a grown woman, wailing in public, blubbering and joking about orgasms like a teenage boy. She takes the key, starts for the elevator, then turns back.

"You're definitely coming?"

Cly assures her she'll be there, tells her to hurry along, the next guest will be arriving soon.

Edith grins. "Okay." She trots off, whistling as she goes, a parting shot. Cly feels the walls constrict along with her ribs, holding their breath until the elevator door closes with a hush and she's gone.

Claire shakes her head. "You are doomed, my love."

Cly nods. "I know, Maman."

When Cly's shift ends, she heads first to the locker room to change so that, at the very least, she won't have to live with having worn her uniform in a guest's room, a space that is not for her; to enter is a violation.

But when she reaches the locker room, she finds Edith standing outside the door. Cly covers her mouth to stifle a cry.

"What are you doing here?"

The circles under her eyes are even darker, fading out to yellow at the periphery, like bruises. Her voice is tiny. "I wanted to make sure you'd really come."

Cly bows her head, hiding her face for a moment. She is suddenly very tired. "C'mon, before someone sees you." She pulls Edith into the employee stairwell that tunnels from one level to another. They begin the slow climb to the twentieth floor, where Edith's room is. She lags behind, panting.

"Hey, slow down. What's the rush? You taking the stairs two at a time?"

Cly turns, glares at her. She hates Edith now. "If someone finds us, I'm not going to be the only one in trouble."

Edith laughs, then falls silent. She picks up the pace a little. Cly wonders how she even found the staircase, let alone got through the door, which can only be opened with an employee ID. She decides it's better not to ask, not only to keep Edith from talking and making more noise, slowing them down further, but to avoid complicity in whatever Edith did to gain access to the inner hive of the hotel.

Miraculously, they reach the twentieth floor without crossing anyone's path.

The hall is deserted, numbers painted in gold on all the doors, tiny, hidden lights illuminating each one, like the entries to individually-wrapped heavens. The carpet is plush, a soft beige that silences their footsteps.

As soon as the door shuts behind them, Edith erupts, all her complaints rushing out in a jumble of curses. Cly stands there, arms at her sides. She tries to respond, but Edith is thundering, spit flying. No one can hear, Cly tells herself. Edith's voice swells to a gale. Cly covers her ears. Finally, exhausted, Edith collapses on the bed with a sigh.

It's only then that Cly thinks to take stock of the room, its colors and furnishings. The walls are a pale yellow, like cake, the carpet and duvet beige, white curtains at the large window overlooking the roof of an apartment building nearby and the street below. The bed is huge and laden with pillows. On the wall opposite is a giant flat-screen TV. Cly knows the TV menu controls many of the room's amenities, though she's never seen it up close. Below stands a dresser, a white moth orchid on top with a blank virgin face, quietly observing. It's just an ordinary room. And yet there is a sense of anticipation, a current of air, though there are no visible vents. What if there are cameras in the rooms? She shakes her head, banishes the thought. Yet she's trembling.

"In a city," Claire might say, "you are never alone. There is always someone watching." She herself is always watching.

"But not here," Cly insists under her breath and her mother gives her a pitying look.

"What?" Edith sits up.

Cly goes to the window and looks out. Her silhouette in the glass is superimposed over the streets like a figure in a collage, the cityscape rendered abstract in squares of light and neon scrawls of cursive, dotted with bright orbs, like so many small moons. On the day of The Accident, a man jumped out of a window. It wasn't this room, it happened on a different side of the building. The window was much like this one, though its glass was breakable. It could be opened. She decides to tell Edith about this, about the man she saw lying on top of someone's car, parts of him so broken as to be unrecognizable while others remained intact, familiar, and how she marveled at that, could not tear herself away from looking at what gravity had taken only a moment to do to him. She couldn't stop staring at what he had so irrevocably done to himself.

"Why are you telling me this?"

Cly stares out the window, watches cars sliding up and down the street. Hidden in the dark are pedestrians on the sidewalks, carrying things, pushing things, talking on their phones. "He'd lost a child." Whatever the hotel revealed to him in his room, he couldn't bear it.

Edith goes quiet. Cly turns, faces her. "You didn't know, did you?"

Edith is stricken, her lips pulled in tight. She doesn't move or speak.

Cly turns back to the window. "But your husband did. I guess that's why he sends you here."

Cly feels something grip the back of her head but before she can register what it is—that it's Edith's hand in her hair—her forehead hits the window hard, the impact reverberating through her skull. She staggers back, then spins around, puts a hand to her head, her mouth open, only to find Edith right on top of her, hands raised, gritting her teeth, eyes hard, the whites shining. Does Edith know the glass is unbreakable?

"You're crazy."

"I told you, I told you my loss. I invited you in. And this is what you do with me?"

"You didn't tell me anything. I found out for myself."

Cly moves fast toward the door but Edith blocks her path, grabs her by both arms and kisses her hard on the mouth. Cly tastes blood. She's not sure whose it is.

"Fuck you." Edith's crying, tears fall into her mouth, drip onto her raggedy sweatshirt. "I love you."

Cly doesn't respond. She opens the door, loosing Edith's wails upon the hallway for just a moment, before the door closes behind her and snuffs them out. Cly turns back. Did she really just pass through that door? She considers the unknowable interior she's entered, touched. Defiled. For Edith. She could be banned from the hotel forever because of her, a price not at all worth paying. She sucks in air through her teeth. Her chest burns as she heads toward the stairwell.

PART II

I

I had a job interview at the sex hotel called The Red Orchid, which was supposed to sound vaguely Japanese. There was something slightly foreign about orchids, with their flowers that looked like something else—insects, aliens. Their care involved expense and precision. And red was self-explanatory, the color of secret interiors: hearts, blood, viscera. I had a fondness for hotels, their grandiosity and cheap secrets. In New York, there were hotels of all rank, from the frightening to the opulent. There were even some for dogs, but they all served the same, broad-spectrum purpose, with shared lobby bathrooms and room service carts lumbering down the halls. They catered to tourists, crowded into rooms smelling of rotten bananas from the children's breakfast. Each one was noisy, mundane. Meanwhile The Red Orchid had turned the Japanese-style love hotel—with its pneumatic tubes and vending machines full of tentacle vibrators and butt plugs—into something stylish and sleek. So that morning, I left the small Brooklyn studio I shared with two other queers, our beds divided by shower curtains hung from the ceiling, bought some burnt, gritty coffee at a bodega outside the station, and took the subway into the city. I was headed to The Red Orchid to apply myself to something menial, where no one would notice me and I could explore the hotel freely. I had student loans to pay back; I'd graduated from an expensive college in the city that my mother hated.

"Have you seen the kids there?" she said when she found out where I wanted to go. "They all look depressed."

"It's a highly ranked school," my father offered. He rarely contradicted her, but he was pleased I was excited about a college, any college, and didn't want to discourage me.

"Look at these classes. 'Poetry in the indigenous oral tradition?' What does that even mean? You can't write poetry without a written language." Of course my mother knew exactly what that meant; she was college-educated herself, and a voracious reader.

"It's just so queer, everything about this school is queer," she muttered. By "queer" she meant "weird." It did no good to correct her; she only said it more.

"It's what Jaime wants," my father said. "Whatever school Jaime feels is best is Jaime's choice." He accepted the conversion from my first to middle name easily enough, but a change in pronouns was beyond him, so he went through verbal gymnastics to avoid having to use any at all. It was exhausting to listen to and irritated my mother to no end.

"What about the parents' opinion here? We get no say?" As if she represented both parents, or her vote counted double— the Mother vote.

But I didn't get in anywhere else—because I never sent in the applications, a detail I failed to mention to my mother—

so my father drove us down to the city. I sat buried in the back amongst my small hoard of belongings, plus a brand new microwave, my mother in front, nervous about my father's driving, digging her fingernails into her seat the whole way. The dorm room had bunk beds and a linoleum floor. My mother cried as she made up my bed for me, even though she was contemptuous of tears.

I sighed with relief once they were gone. My life could begin now, I thought.

I enrolled in writing classes where my teachers drew diagrams and talked about guns going off. They instructed my classmates and me to show each other things without saying them. Most of the stories were terrible regardless.

"It's okay not to have a real job now, but you'll need one by the time you're thirty," one professor told the class. Most of us were full-time students. All we had were un-real jobs. Our instructor was in their forties, I guessed. It was unclear whether teaching counted as a real job; writing obviously did not.

The best instruction came from the city itself. It was full of basement readings and interminable open mics, ancient, musty bookstores with aisles too small to pass through, the books stacked three volumes deep. I read and scribbled, lingering over meals at humid hole-in-the-walls where the waitresses were as brusque as civil servants. There were diners serving vegan BLTs and limp, greasy fries all night, Polish bakeries and shops with Turkish delight and bins of rice in every color, bodegas displaying shining fruits and orange flowers under plastic awnings on every corner. There were people, of all sizes and looks, everywhere. They glared, shouted insults, whistled, but mostly ignored each other. I was skinny and white, with a neutral haircut, plainly dressed. "You dress like a bird watcher without binoculars," my freshman year roommate said. My notebook and I traveled freely, recording it all.

"Where's your glitter, girl?" a towering queen once called to me from across the street. I was in the Village at night, lost. I froze. Girl? She winked. I didn't know if she thought I was actually a girl, or a twink. It didn't matter, sparkle was gender neutral. I wrote a flash piece about it.

"Are you writing?" My mother asked on our weekly phone calls. "Don't tell me what it's about." She assumed I wrote about strange sexual acts and proclivities, or whatever it was I did with my friends who dreamed of becoming teachers and nonprofit founders.

Lately, I spent my days applying for jobs and my nights hunched over a blank, glowing screen. Meanwhile, my mother was unsubtly hinting at cutting me off if I couldn't soon make a career of writing, even though I'd told my parents it would likely be years before I made real headway, that perhaps I'd never make much money or receive acclaim, that sometimes the best a writer can hope for is to be lauded posthumously, then inflicted upon bored high school students. My mother kept books like pets, but she knew nothing about publishing.

My brother Gabe, who in grade school sold me out to his classmates to increase his own social capital, now worked in finance. His life and identity fit tidily into pre-labeled boxes; he was steadily acquiring all the accessories necessary to achieve proper adulthood and had become the kind of guy who talked about sports with strangers, gave people unironic thumbs-up.

Gabe could help me find a job, my mother said. Except there was no way I could work in finance. But my mother didn't understand that, either, because my sibling and I both knew how to use a computer and as far as she was concerned, that was the same thing.

Meanwhile my father bought a kit to put together a toy plane. He also enjoyed 3D puzzles of historic castles. He was working on one now that was supposed to turn into the Tower of London. My mother told me about it the last time we talked on the phone, which was on my birthday a few months earlier. By now he'd have finished the puzzle.

"An old man building a toy," she said. Even my father needed to grow up.

The hotel lobby was glass-doored, orchids everywhere: round-petaled phalaenopsis with their vaginal lips and cymbidiums with protruding, clitoral noses; spotted, splay-limbed *Renanthera monachica*, all perched atop little marble-topped pedestals that had been set up throughout the room. In keeping with the hotel's name, the orchids were all shades of red, from carmine to purple. The lobby looked like a greenhouse on Valentine's Day. The air even felt slightly humid. Misty.

A little fountain burbled behind the check-in desk, which gleamed with high polish. The marble floor shone as well. Plush, white couches, vulnerable to stains, balanced on brass orbs instead of feet, clouds among all the red flowers.

At the desk stood a petite young person with large, dark eyes, creamy skin, and a mass of black, shining hair pulled back carelessly in a clip. Her uniform was modest: black button-down shirt with a red orchid embroidered on the chest, just above her nametag, and matching black slacks. Yet with the fountain behind her, she looked like a priestess, awaiting pilgrims upon whom she'd bestow room keys. Her nametag read "Adrienne." I didn't think she would be the one to interview me for a job but I'd still have to talk to her to get to the person who would. Each encounter with a stranger required an exhausting negotiation of perception. Would she be openly hostile, or overcompensate to the point of obsequiousness? Who could say? She looked like a vestal virgin. I told myself she was really just an ordinary person, someone who had needed a job and found one. In a sense, she was just like me. All the same, I would have to force the words out, and my voice might come out too loud or too quiet or at the wrong register. I was thinking about this, how my voice sometimes betrayed me, another way in which the body required vigilance and management, when I realized I was just standing at the desk, staring at Adrienne, not saying anything, and she was staring back at me with her faint smile, waiting patiently for me to speak.

"Can I help you?" she said in a way that suggested she'd already asked me this question but I hadn't answered. I flushed and started pawing at the stubborn cowlick at the back of my head, which I knew Adrienne couldn't see, but its constant presence shamed me all the same, the flaw in what would otherwise be my best feature. I had no choice but to tolerate being undermined by this coquettish flip, offering a peek of my pink scalp beneath my hair, fluttering in the slightest breeze like downy duck feathers. No matter what I did, I could never be rid of it.

I cleared my throat. It was as confident a throat-clearing as I could achieve. I asked for the manager.

"Certainly," Adrienne said, reaching for the phone. She didn't question me further. Probably she was relieved to pass me off to someone else.

A short man in a suit appeared and smiled at me, shook my hand heartily, looking not so much at me as through me. His hands were small for his frame. He introduced himself and gave me his full name, but it was only the first that I caught, the last name lost to my ear, something with a lot of vowels, maybe Greek. He had a slight accent I couldn't place. Then for some reason, I thought of Morocco. Edison from Morocco. I'd never met anyone named Edison before. I didn't ask if he was named after Thomas Edison because most likely everyone asked him that.

Edison ushered me into his office, a windowless closet just off the lobby with a paper calendar taped to the wall behind the desk. Two years out of date, the calendar displayed the proud neon-yellow, bikini-clad butt of a model who had been caught mid-turn by the camera as she gripped a tall, thick, sweaty bottle of beer. There was nothing else on the walls, the desk free of all clutter or decoration except for a single framed photo, which was turned toward Edison. I imagined it was a picture of his wife, or maybe his child. Or his mother.

Edison informed me the hotel was ten stories high with only eight to ten rooms on each floor. The building was historic and had changed hands several times.

"We've got spots on the kitchen crew, and janitorial, which is distinct from housekeeping," he said. "But first . . ." He gestured grandly toward the door, offering me a tour.

The ceilings were low, the floors creaked, yet the first floor hallways were coated with fresh beige paint flecked with gold and the soft burgundy carpet appeared new. As we walked, motion-sensored lights came to life.

"Here's the elevator," Edison pointed at a pair of gilded doors. They went bing! and parted smoothly, music spilling out. There was no one inside.

We moved farther down the hall. "Would you like to see one of the rooms?" Edison paused. The doorknob was made of crystal.

"Of course," I said, hoping he'd leave the door open.

Edison turned a big brass key in the lock and I found myself staring at the interior of an airplane with rows of plain dark blue seats. The walls were covered in heavy plastic siding, inlaid with a row of robin's egg windows. Some had more clouds than others. In one, you could see land, soft quilt squares of green and brown. Above the seats, shelves jutted out of the walls to form overhead compartments.

"Go ahead, look around." Edison stood by the door, which he did leave open out of courtesy, hands clasped under his belly.

Each row only had two armrests, one at each end. I pressed the recline button and the whole row fell back about twenty degrees farther than actual airline seats would go.

The finishing touch was the bathroom. I entered through a tiny lavatory door at the back of the room, complete with a little green slot above the doorknob that said "vacant." Inside was a real toilet with a real flushing mechanism, but the sink was metal-lined, the whole thing so cramped, the lighting so unflattering, that it did indeed feel like an actual airplane bathroom, though fortunately it did not smell like one.

"So let me tell you a bit more about working here," Edison said as we exited the room. "We do things a little differently. Housekeeping keeps the rooms clean, while janitorial . . ." A siren interrupted him. He paused, ready to continue. Then we heard a loud shriek.

"Excuse me." Edison hustled toward the lobby, his hands curling and uncurling at his sides.

I followed.

We found twenty or so people rushing about, calling to each other, yelling into their phones, their free hands waving, gesturing excitedly, knocking over orchids. The floor was a mess of flower pot shards, bark and clumps of hairy moss, and trampled blossoms turned to menstrual stains, along with dropped aprons, coats, totes and messenger bags, a few suitcases—small ones, the kind you'd take on a weekend trip. I thought for a minute that the building was on fire, but no alarm had sounded.

To my right, the glass double doors I'd passed through only minutes before swished open and closed. A group of five people tried to exit at once and their bodies got plastered together. For a moment they were stuck in the doorway, crushed and wriggling, wailing as they tried to free themselves at once, the people who had come up behind them standing there, waiting, till finally they were squeezed out in a rush onto the street, the first two falling to the ground. Of those behind them, two more fell on top of the pile, one clambered over. Then they all ran. Three people who'd been waiting their turn went out one by one. I realized then that most everyone was in uniform. Why didn't they just leave through another door, then? Something was terribly wrong.

As I looked out at the street, my gaze drifted past the heads of the people rushing this way and that up to the impassive, pigeon-stained faces of the buildings, then farther up to the rooftops, and that was when I saw it.

It was a cloud. And yet it wasn't. It was a mass, thick and gray, an animal's coat, a shaggy wolf slowly consuming the expanse of the sky, devouring the light. A thing God had been keeping back in his stable until now, eerily familiar, like meeting one's own inevitable doom. My throat tightened.

"Holy shit," said Edison, and I realized he was standing beside me, though a moment later he dashed off, waving at his dwindling staff, which did nothing to staunch the flow of bodies streaming out of the hotel's front doors, till the last one slipped past and disappeared.

II

All of a sudden, the lobby was strangely quiet. And dark. Adrienne was behind the desk, the phone pressed to her ear, waiting for something. Edison hovered over her.

"How many guests haven't checked out yet?" He sounded frantic.

Adrienne rolled her eyes. "Hold on." She scanned her screen. "Only a few. There's someone right here in the Garden Room, looks like." She pointed down the hall.

"Okay, okay, good, leave them," Edison said.

"Shouldn't we let them know what's going on?"

"What *is* going on?" Edison aimed a remote at a TV I'd failed to notice. A morning talk-show host smiled down at us with ersatz benevolence. She opened her mouth to speak just as Edison changed the channel.

I glanced down the hall. "You said someone's right here? Wouldn't they hear the commotion?"

Adrienne shook her head at me without looking up from her screen. "Soundproofed rooms."

Soundproofing, of course. How clever. "I can go knock. Should I go knock?"

She ignored me.

"I'll go," I declared and headed in the direction Adrienne had pointed.

Except I didn't know which door to knock on. Then I noticed one was slightly ajar. I pushed it and it glided open silently to reveal a room full of plants, including an apple tree with a basket of fruit at its feet and a crown that grazed the skylight. This had to be the Garden Room. The glass looked translucent but I couldn't tell from the floor if it really was so, or if the fog pressing down on it made it appear that way. Or maybe it was dirty with soot. Regardless, the window was a square of gloom on a ceiling painted to look like a clear sky, with glittering butterflies and hummingbirds suspended from wires. Picnic weather. A clock shaped like an owl checked off each second, its eyes sleepily rolling back and forth. It was only 10:30 a.m. The carpet was coarse and resembled artificial scrub grass. The bed was round, nestled in a wicker frame like a bird's nest, the pillows shaped like eggs, the comforter made up of strips of felt in varying shades of brown and beige. And then I realized with a start that someone was there, asleep in the nest, a shapely leg thrown over the covers. From what I could tell, she was naked. I tried to retreat without waking her, but she sat up, flashing me a small, pert breast as she rubbed her eyes, yawned. Then she saw me. She didn't say anything. My hand was still on the doorknob.

"I'm so sorry." I looked at the carpet beneath the nest and noticed a condom wrapper lying there amongst some apple cores and small, torn up bits of what looked like wax paper.

The woman was watching me, bemused, unfazed by a stranger entering her room. She made no move to cover herself.

I cleared my throat. "There's an emergency."

Without a word, she stood up, a silver charm on her wrist catching the light as she reached for her clothes, slung across the back of a chair made of twigs, and began dressing, her back to me. Her ass was tattooed, a constellation in dark blue inked across her left cheek. I wondered which constellation it was. It looked like maybe Orion. She stepped on a piece of the wax paper and it stuck to her foot. A diamond pattern had been pressed into it, like snakeskin. Maybe it really was snakeskin. Then I realized I was still standing there and shut the door. I rushed back down the hall, face burning, watching my sneakers to anchor myself.

The TV was on mute. A big-breasted news anchor in a hot pink blazer mouthed words with plump, shining lips, her skin stretched too tightly across her skull for a ripple of emotion. Ribbons of text scrolled across the lower half of the screen. They said something like, "Mysterious cloud engulfs NYC, mass panic ensues." Not exactly that. Maybe they didn't use the word "engulf." Or "panic."

Click-clack. It was the woman I had come upon in the bird's nest. She was dressed now in a loose, creamy white blouse and a short, A-line black leather skirt, with bare legs and black peep toe stilettos. She wore no jewelry beside the one, slim bracelet with what I now saw was a single, cat-shaped charm. She didn't have on any makeup that I could detect either, though it seemed she had taken the time to brush her hair, which was lustrous and long, shining in a black cascade over her shoulder. The air thickened around her as my stomach oozed up through my chest and swallowed my heart. She saw me looking at her and smiled slightly, a coy smile for herself, not me. I blushed from forehead to collarbone and shifted my gaze back to the TV. The news had turned to a silent video of a podium with the mayor behind it. A cell phone buzzed once, then three more times in quick succession. I risked a quick glance at the woman from the Garden Room, saw her shaking her head at her phone as one finger danced across the screen. Sighing, she walked over to one of the white couches and sat down. Her gait was slightly pigeon-toed.

I hadn't looked outside since I'd come back downstairs, even though the doors were right there. I moved my head ever so slightly to the side. A little more, with eyes downcast, till I thought I could just get a peek. Then I looked up, fast. At first, I didn't see it and felt a swell of relief. I almost laughed. But then I realized I was staring right at it. Except for a little swath of blue, the cloud had enveloped the entire skyscape. It was too dark, too dense, with a purplish hint of violence in its folds. I imagined this was what a storm looked like on Mars. There were faces in its shadows, stern giants frowning down at us, poised to squash or swallow all.

The bird's nest woman was looking outside, too. Slowly, heels clicking, she made her way over to the glass doors. When she walked, she moved from the shoulder first, her hips following, toes pointed inward. She stood there, looking up, the phone in one hand buzzing every few seconds as she reached up with the other and pressed her palm flat against the glass, fingers splayed. When she turned back toward the room, her wry smile had gone and been replaced by an expression that terrified me far more than the cloud itself. I couldn't know what she saw when she looked up at it, what she knew or imagined that I didn't. Then I noticed a thin strand of white bleeding out from her temple, stark against her black hair. Had that been there before? It must have, I told myself. My heart was beating too fast, blood thrumming in my ears like someone pounding on a door. I thought of my parents in their quaint little kitchen upstate, the tiny, ancient television set my father Harold would prop up on the table if there was something important on and he wanted to watch it during breakfast, my mother frowning, disapproving as always, vigorously scraping a pan from last night's dinner over the sink in the background. Were they watching this? Did they know?

I looked around the room, counting: Adrienne, Edison, the Garden Room guest. Four of us so far. No one was speaking; they were all transfixed by the TV except Adrienne, who was staring stonily ahead, lips sucked in. I couldn't tell what she was looking at, if anything at all. The Garden Room woman sat on the couch, legs crossed, leather skirt hiked up and twisted around her hips as she continued texting. Slowly, I shuffled across the lobby, then positioned myself a few feet behind the couch, casually leaning on one leg, my chin tilted upward so I could see the TV. I snuck a glance at her phone. I couldn't read the text, only saw the contact was "Mother." I felt around in my pockets, searching for my own cell phone. Had anyone tried to call me? Then I realized I'd left the phone in my apartment. I could see it clearly, sitting primly on my pillow. I glanced back at her phone and saw the chain of messages growing longer and longer. How many texts had she exchanged within the last ten minutes? Thirty?

As if she'd heard me, she looked over her shoulder at me and fluttered her lashes. I'd been caught. I blushed, then cleared my throat, deciding to go with it.

"Why doesn't she just call you?"

She paused, as if considering how to feel about this question. Then she smirked at me and sighed, rolling her eyes at the same time for a combined effect of exhausted exasperation. "Because she doesn't want to be a bother."

I felt myself smile. "I'm sorry I . . ." I didn't know what to say.

She waved me off. Her nails were glossy. Short, black cherry squares. There was something inscribed on her charm: a name, it looked like.

"It's fine," she said, and in that moment, I was grateful to her because it most certainly wasn't fine, though of course it wasn't my fault the door had been unlocked and ajar. But nothing was at all fine about today, and I was appreciative of her calm in this moment, the very ordinary thing she was doing—texting her mother—and the ordinary conversation we were having about it, even if her face had shaken me to my core only a few minutes ago.

"I was supposed to have left already," she murmured. "That bed was just surprisingly comfortable." She thrust a slender hand at me. I shook it gently. "I'm Zosiah."

She was Jewish? Again, I blushed.

"Can I ask you what it was like, sleeping in that room?"

"I didn't really sleep much." She smiled, then paused. "It was weird. I thought it would just be kind of kitschy and over the top, not necessarily sexy. But it felt very real. And strange at the same time."

"How so?"

She shook her head. "I can't explain it."

I wanted to ask about the snakeskin but couldn't think of a tactful way to mention it. Meanwhile, the TV got unmuted and the anchorwoman with the motionless face and torpedo breasts suddenly had a voice to tell us she knew nothing, while issuing cautions at seemingly timed intervals to stay indoors, stay inside, don't go out until . . . . Until what?

III

A couple appeared in the lobby. They were holding hands, giggling and nuzzling. When they saw us, their smiles fell away and they let go of one another.

At the same time, a pale, well-muscled man in uniformed coveralls—"Jason," his nametag said—materialized behind the desk. Had he been there all along? He had shaggy, sable hair that nearly hid his eyes, and he was leaning over Adrienne, whispering to her. She ignored him.

"Hey." He looked up at the new couple. "You two need to go sit down," he barked, pointing to one of the couches. His voice had a touch of Jersey in it. I could tell he wanted Adrienne to see he was in charge. She went on ignoring him.

The women gaped at him, stunned, their eyes wide with alarm. Without a word, they walked over to the vacant couch opposite Zosiah and sat down. Then they looked around without moving their heads, eyes darting about like fish in a bowl, waiting for something to happen.

I felt eyes on me. It was Jason, looking me over from across the room. I knew he was trying to decide whether to treat me like a woman, or something else, something worse. It happened every time I approached a door: who would open it and who would wait passively for it to be opened? Cis men scowled, territorial, clinging to door handles like Moses' tablet.

Edison headed over to the couple on the couch. "Hi." He extended his hand. "I'm Edison, the manager." He shook their hands while they looked on, bewildered. One was white with close-cropped, blond hair—a New England mom's haircut— and had a plain, doughy face. She said her name was Calle. She was wearing clogs. The other, Ruth, was a little younger than her lover, or maybe they were the same age, she was just softer, with freckles dotting her light brown skin and copper curls pulled back in a ponytail. She had large, dark eyes that peered about mournfully.

"What's going on?" Calle asked.

"We need to stay indoors, something's happening outside," Edison began. Nothing else he said made very much sense. Finally, he sighed and pointed at the glass doors, though really he was pointing at the sky. They turned around and looked. Then they got up and slowly made their way to the door. Outside, a siren whooped. I glanced at Jason. He was watching them, twitching a little, sweating.

"We should seal ourselves in," he grumbled. Acid rushed up my throat. I closed my eyes for a just a moment. Suddenly, I was huddled with my family under a blanket in the living room in the dark, the wind whistling. A storm had taken out the power lines, covered the windows, buried the house in the snow. All night, my brother sat up, bored, jiggling his leg, poking me at intervals with a bony stick of a finger to keep me awake, too. That was how he entertained himself. My mother moaned in her sleep.

Calle and Ruth stood in front of the door, their backs to us, hands at their sides. Then, slowly, they raised them up to their faces and held them there as they stood staring at the sky. I didn't look. I knew it was there, that it was *still* there. When they finally turned around, I averted my eyes to avoid their faces. I knew what they would look like.

Jason spoke again, louder this time. "We should seal ourselves in."

Edison nodded. "You and I can take care of that."

"Seal us in how?" asked Calle. "Is that really necessary?"

"Well, on the news . . ." Edison began.

She cut him off. "I have a son." Ruth put a hand on her shoulder. The rest stared. "I can't be trapped in here because I have a son." She was flushed.

"Where is your son now?" Edison asked.

I glanced at Zosiah. She was still texting.

Calle was shaking. Her teeth clacked. "At school," she said. "I think. I don't know. How am I supposed to know?" She doubled over, covering her head with her hands as Ruth shushed her, rubbing her back in circles.

Zosiah suddenly looked up, taking in the new arrivals. She got up from her couch and sat down next to the couple. "Do you have a phone on you? You can use mine if there's someone you need to call."

"I don't know who to call. My neighbor was going to take him to school so his fa—" She stopped herself, began again, speaking fast. "When did this happen? When did this start?" She looked to each of us for an answer. Her face was swollen like an overripe fruit.

I stepped forward and gave her my best estimate, telling her what time I had arrived at the hotel and around when we first noticed the cloud. She thanked me and removed a phone from her own pocket.

"I'm Ruth," Calle's companion beamed at me, offered a half-hearted wave.

"Jaime." No one had mentioned pronouns, or used many yet. "They/them," I added too fast, sputtering, swallowing the last consonant. I'd lost my pronoun swagger.

She nodded, still smiling blankly. She probably thought I'd given some odd last name. Then she turned back to Calle, who was jiggling her leg, cell phone pressed to her ear. Ruth began rubbing her shoulders.

Meanwhile, Zosiah had gone back to texting her mother. Jason and Edison were gone, presumably off sealing us in, whatever that meant. They hadn't invited anyone else to join their mission I noted, not that I would've wanted to wander around with them alone. I was uneasy with their de facto authority.

I approached the check-in desk. Adrienne was still there, hunched over, doodling on a pad of hotel stationery. I leaned back against the desk, as if I didn't know she was there. Then I turned to her slowly.

"Do you need to call anyone?"

She kept drawing. Without looking up, she said, "I have a phone." She didn't say it meanly, just matter-of-factly. Her voice was rich, surprisingly deep for a person so young and small.

"What's it like working here?" I asked softly, as if lowering my voice would make the question more pertinent and less prying. I hoped she'd say something insightful, or at least informative.

Adrienne looked up for a second, blinked, then shrugged and went back to her doodle. "I mostly just stand around, waiting for people to check in or out. It's not really that exciting."

"Did you check all these people in?"

"That's confidential, but no. My shift just started."

I nodded, though she didn't see it.

Calle had reached someone, the neighbor, perhaps. She rubbed her forehead, saying, "Yeah, yeah." Ruth was still massaging her shoulders, and Calle endured it with a grimace.

"Where do you live?"

"Queens."

I nodded. There was no one living in this whole city that I really loved, or who loved me in return. The thought was gut-wrenching. Yet whatever happened here, I reasoned, my parents would be fine.

"None of my family lives in the city," I heard myself say. Until recently, my mother's snobbish younger sister Jeanie had lived in the East Village. Once a year she took me to dinner, or "tea." My first year of college, my parents grudgingly accepted her invitation and drove down for a Christmas all together in

Jeanie's "flat," with green boughs framing the doors, quaint, pagan baubles, and bearded little men galore. My mother was nervous, talking nonstop, tugging at the hem of her holiday sweater like a schoolgirl. She only acted that way around her family.

"Isn't your mother an odd one?" My magenta-haired aunt declared. She was wearing a chunky ring the size of her hand. She leaned in close and I smelled the stale wine and onion dip on her breath.

I wanted to record a scrap about living in a city where no one loved you. Where was my bag? I patted my chest. There it was, still slung across my torso, with a beat-up old notebook inside. I'd kept one since I was seven. The oldest were in a box in my parents' attic, those from college on were tucked under my bed. I averaged about one notebook every three months. I began digging around for a pen.

"Excuse me," I said to Adrienne, though she obviously didn't care if this conversation went on or not.

I jogged over to the hallway, just off the lobby. With my back against the wall, I slid down to the floor, stretched out my legs, set the notebook on my thigh and began writing, gripping the pen too hard as usual. My hand had just started to cramp when I heard a voice above me.

"What are you writing?"

I looked up to see Zosiah, peering down at me. "What? Oh, nothing." I imagined her lustrous hair gently brushing against my face. She smiled quizzically at me and nudged me with the toe of her heel. Her top lip was round, with just the barest indentation right in the center.

"You're writing nothing?"

"Just notes. I'm a writer. I'm trying to be a writer."

Zosiah leaned against the wall, then slid down to sit beside me. Her purse, a frumpy, black leather box that looked like it belonged to a much older woman, was slung over one shoulder. "What kind of stuff? Mystery?" She paused, looking me over. "Sci-fi?"

I cleared my throat. "Just fiction."

"Oh." She had nothing to say to that. Most people, I found, had nothing to say to that.

"Is your mother all right?"

Zosiah looked confused for a moment. "Oh, her?" She sighed. "She'll be fine. There's nothing can take her down, that one." As if on cue, her phone buzzed again.

"Does she know where you are?" I asked, without thinking.

Zosiah smiled to herself. "She follows my every move. She used to read my diary when I was in high school. I planted a decoy once, but she figured it out and grounded me."

"Did she give you that bracelet?"

Zosiah looked down at it, wrapped her hand around the silver bangle, covering it.

"No," she said softly. She smiled with her lips pressed together, then looked away. I waited for her to elaborate; she didn't.

"Zosiah. That's a beautiful name."

"It's not my real name. My original one, I mean." She touched her face. "Born in Korea, raised on brisket."

"Oh." I wanted to give a smart reply: "born upstate, raised on . . ." Latkes? My mother never made latkes, or even challah. I said I was from upstate but now lived in Brooklyn. She nodded. Her mother had lived near Rochester for a time. Then Zosiah told me about her mother's roast chicken, how she insisted it brought people luck and dropped the cooked birds on her daughter's stoop once a week.

"I'm convinced she spits on it, for luck."

I'd never seen my mother spit, not once.

Zosiah's mother lived alone, her husband having died a long time ago. Now her sole ambition in life was to see her daughter get married and have children, so her husband could die, her children could grow up, and she too would know what it was like to be left all alone.

"Do you have a . . . partner?" I asked.

Zosiah smiled like I was missing something so I smiled back, confused, until suddenly I got it. Someone else had paid for the room, someone who had left without her. I blushed.

"Maybe someday," she said. "When I get too old for all this. Right now it's too much. My mother keeps reminding me," she wagged her finger with mock consternation and her bracelet slid over her wrist, " 'You won't look like this forever! You better get married before you get cellulite and your tits drop!' " She laughed. The sound was delightful.

I put my notebook back in my bag. I just wanted her to keep talking with me, like traumatized airline passengers on a turbulent flight, blurting out our whole lives to strangers who weren't strangers anymore because they were in this, whatever this was. I looked for that small strand of white in her hair. It was still there.

"Did you go to school in the city?"

"Nope, Mount Holyoke." She beamed.

"Really?"

"Yup, I was the big dyke on campus. Fauxhawk and everything." She squinted and laughed at me. "Don't look so surprised."

"Oh, no, I believe you."

"I had swagger!" she insisted. I could see her in thick soled boots and jeans, feet set apart, though slightly turned in, winking at terrified coeds as she marched around campus. I would've blushed, too.

"What did your mother say?"

She looked away. "That it was a phase." Zosiah shrugged. "I guess she was kinda right." She turned her face back to mine. She wanted me to know this about her, that she'd occupied a world that intersected with mine, or what she perceived mine to be.

"Then I dropped out," she went on.

"I majored in creative writing," I offered.

"Oh, that's worse than English."

I couldn't disagree.

A major in English was even more of a conversation killer than fiction. Zosiah went off to find a bathroom. She didn't ask me to come along so I didn't offer to join her. I didn't think about whether or not she'd be safe wandering around by herself. When I reached the threshold between the hall and the lobby, I saw Ruth, Calle, and Adrienne gathered together on the floor in front of the couches, the TV above them back on mute. The room was even darker; they'd hung bed sheets over the doors, blocking the view of the cloud. They were huddled close, talking in low, conspiratorial tones, and I hung back for a moment, watching Adrienne hold their attention, how she sat on her feet, her shoes kicked off. She took their hands, one in each of hers, as if offering them benediction. I reached again for my notebook.

Then I heard something behind me. I turned to see Zosiah racing toward me, her face flushed, mouth open. She had her phone in one hand, her stilettos in the other. Without them, she was much shorter. Her wide, bare feet padded against the carpet.

"My phone," she panted. She pushed past me, rushed into the lobby. "My phone! My phone isn't working!" she announced to the room.

Startled, the others looked up, then snatched their phones from their pockets. Adrienne made her way back to the desk. For a moment, they stood staring at the little screens, fingers failing to gently nudge them back to life.

"The towers must be down," Ruth said, glancing at Calle, who began to pace before the door, her arms crossed over her chest. Just then, a rash of sirens went off outside. A moment later, I heard the screech of tires, followed by a crash. I looked toward the double doors, but I didn't move.

"Landline's down," Adrienne informed us, placing the handset back in the cradle. For a moment, no one said anything.

Calle had stopped pacing. Her arms still crossed, she studied the bed linens covering the glass.

"Calle . . ." Ruth warned as she reached for the sheet.

"I just want to see."

"No." Ruth grabbed at her hand.

"I just want to see!"

"No!" Ruth wrapped her in a bear hug, pinning Calle's arms to her sides. "Don't look!"

"I just wanna see if it's still there!" Calle wriggled and flexed, struggling to break free.

"Hey." It was Edison. "What's going on?"

Everyone looked up. Their expressions showed both relief and resignation, a look I would describe as, "Oh, the men are back." I hunched my shoulders. Ruth relaxed her hold, and Calle slipped away.

Edison had emerged from the hallway to the left of the check-in desk. He was holding a bedsheet. Next to him stood Jason with a stack of linens.

"The phones are dead," Adrienne informed them. "Landline and cells."

Jason shook his head as if to say *I told you so*.

"Okay, let's everybody sit down," Edison gestured toward the couches. We reorganized them into a circle and I flashed back to college seminars where everyone was a little too comfortable, a little too sleepy, the couches too soft, all of us well-fed and assured of the value of our opinions.

Calle went back to pacing in front of the door. Ruth called out to her in a sing-song, but she just shook her head, arms crossed again over her chest.

"It's fine," Edison told Ruth, but I noticed Jason was chewing his lip, eyes trained on Calle. What was he going to do if she tried to open that door?

I glanced at Zosiah, sitting next to me, cradling her cell phone like a dead bird. She was wearing sunglasses now, big dark frames that hid half her face. Maybe she was crying behind them.

With excruciating slowness, we went around one by one and shared our names. Edison went first, introducing himself as the manager of the hotel, just in case any of us didn't know that. He told us where he lived, that he was a Yankees fan but preferred soccer, that Barcelona was his team.

Last was Jason. All he did was repeat his name while staring at Adrienne, who was picking at a piece of dead skin on her finger.

"What do you do here?" I asked, and Jason turned to me, eyebrows disappearing under his pop star hair, big chin jutting out. He took his time looking me over again so I could feel his gaze through my clothes, all over my skin, taking in the body underneath, laughing. I shuddered but tried to hide it.

"I work in maintenance. I keep things at the hotel running smoothly."

"Jason provides some assistance with security measures," Edison said. What did security have to do with maintenance?

"That's right." He nodded.

"Really?" Adrienne added flatly, "is that what you call bouncing drunk people?"

Jason pretended not to hear her. "Edison and I just stoppered all the windows, all the vents. If it's poison or a toxin or something out there . . ." he pointed at the door. Calle stopped pacing. "We've done all we can to keep it from getting in here." He pointed at the floor.

At that, we went quiet. Zosiah glanced up from her dead phone. Ruth clasped her hands as she surveyed the room, opened her mouth a few times to speak, then thought better of it.

"Look," Jason went on, sitting up a little higher, "they said on the news to stay indoors. That's what we're going to do."

The same newscaster appeared on the silenced TV, the same text trawling across the bottom of the screen, plus something about the president and his great concern for all of us. Uh huh.

"Until *they* know, we don't go." Jason smiled at his accidental rhyme. He flashed his teeth. I looked at Adrienne. She worked at the hotel, too, but that didn't seem to matter. She was staring at something I couldn't see, paying no attention to any of us.

Zosiah was frowning and picking at her nails, her eyes still hidden behind her sunglasses. Meanwhile Ruth was watching Calle intently as she continued pacing, tossing her head now and then like a bull. The skin covering her face and neck was inflamed. Calle scratched it vigorously. Ruth cast a surreptitious glance at the TV. Slowly she repositioned herself like a plant stretching toward the sunlight till finally she was facing it, her head tilted back so she could see the screen, Calle likely still visible in her peripheral vision. I glanced over at Jason, expecting he was still keeping an eye on Calle, but instead found he was studying Ruth, his eyes roving over her body. Ruth didn't appear to notice, but she had to feel it. I glanced at the TV again, checking to see if the scrolling text had changed. It hadn't, but there were more people on the screen now.

"How can it be that they still don't know anything?" Ruth asked herself softly, with genuine incredulity. The others heard her. Zosiah looked up, pushed her sunglasses to the crown of her head. I expected her face to be puffy and red from weeping, but her eyes were clear.

We all turned our attention to the TV. Edison removed the remote from his pocket and unmuted the host as she was introducing a few expert guests, the camera panning over a tight, awkward face with each intro. There were three of them, all white men. One of them wore a bow tie; another was in a suit, with a well-trimmed beard. The third wore a military uniform. The guy in the suit was a bioterrorism expert, the one in uniform the weapons expert, of course. Why did they need both of them? The one in the bow tie had a doctorate in something I didn't catch, something to do with ecology, climatology. He was a proper scientist. That one went first, explaining why the cloud was unusual, though he didn't say anything that wasn't obvious just from looking out the window.

"So, this is man-made?" The host aimed her breasts at him.

"Well, we don't know that for sure."

"But is it naturally occurring or not? Have you seen this before?"

"Well . . ."

Now the one in the suit cut him off. For the moment, the cloud's composition was more important than its origins, he said. "This could be a weapon unlike anything we've ever seen."

The other weapons guy nodded in agreement and opened his mouth to speak, but the host got in first.

"Have there been any reported effects? Is anyone sick? Have there been any confirmed casualties?"

At that, the men began to shout all at once, waving their fingers in each other's faces. The host sat there, unmoved, nodding intermittently, as the guests went on gesticulating and hollering.

Finally, the bioterrorism guy got in a few coherent words. "It's still too early to know the effects," he said. "We might see consequences from this in another 48 hours, in a week, a year. We just don't know. We need time to collect data."

"Whatever it is, we need to ensure citizens are protected and that we get this thing dispersed as soon as possible." The weapons man in uniform tapped the desk with his knuckles.

The bioterrorism expert turned on the weapons guy. "Safety measures have been put into effect. In terms of 'dispersing' this phenomenon, how do you propose we accomplish that?"

The ecologist tried to insert himself into the conversation but was shouted down by the two weapons men. And on it went.

Calle was sitting on the floor, staring down at the tiles. Periodically, she scratched at her neck and forearms. Her arms were red now, too. Looking at her skin made me itch. I couldn't help myself, I began digging at my own neck, then my arms. Zosiah stared at me.

Jason asked Edison for the remote. Then he stood up, aimed the device at the TV, and with a grunt, shut it off. A chorus of protests broke out.

"We're not getting anything out of this." Jason stood over us, waving the remote. "They don't know anything."

Calle and I scratched at ourselves like dogs. My whole body felt like one irritated sleeve of skin. Out of the corner of my eye, I saw Zosiah scratching, too, digging at her elbow with her short, dark nails.

Calle stood up. "If they don't know anything, if no one's died, then why can't we leave?"

We all turned to Jason.

"If you leave, you compromise the integrity of this entire building." His face glowed with sweat.

Compromise the integrity. It was the kind of thing my brother would say. He lived in Connecticut now and voted Republican. My mother, who didn't discuss politics, claimed he was thinking of buying a home.

I imagined Jason somewhere in New Jersey in a ramshackle house he'd inherited from his grandmother. Or maybe a duplex. When his neighbors fought, his grandmother's old china figurines trembled in their case.

Calle shifted her weight from foot to foot. She had come to a decision. "Fuck this." She wheeled around and began pawing at the sheet covering the doors.

"No!" Ruth rushed at her and grabbed her arm. Jason and Edison were close behind. Then, a thump. I looked at the floor, thinking a cell phone had fallen. There was nothing there. Calle let go of the door and Ruth let go of Calle. Edison and Jason stood there, hands raised like spotters at the gym. Another thump. It sounded like something had hit the window.

"What was that?" Zosiah said.

Trembling, Ruth reached up and pulled back the sheet.

IV

A dead pigeon was lying on its back just outside the door, legs sticking straight up like a parody of death. I had distinctly heard two thumps but saw only one bird.

"It's just a pigeon," I said.

Jason chuckled. Ruth cooed sadly and covered her mouth. Zosiah smiled a little half-smile. Then her face went blank. The room grew strangely quiet. We couldn't see more than a few feet past the door, not that there was anything to see.

I suddenly understood why there was a sheet over the doors. It wasn't to protect us from the sight of the world out there, it was to make that world seem farther away than it really was. Anything at all could come out of the cloud and rush toward us, press up against the glass, and there would be no shield from that horror.

And then, something did come flying out of the fog, torpedoing right at us, though we couldn't see it till it hit the window with a sickening "thwack," wings splayed, beady eye fixed. We all screamed as the bird made contact with the door, which shuddered from the impact. Then the bird dropped out of sight.

There was a bright streak of blood on the glass. This time, no one laughed.

Suddenly, the door shuddered again as three more smacked the window at once. Zosiah screamed. A deluge of hideous thumps followed, a hailstorm of birds. Was the door locked? Ruth heard my thoughts, began frantically fiddling with the lock until Jason rushed over and pushed her aside.

"It's already secured!"

"Close the curtain!" Zosiah cried. She had her hands over her ears, her eyes pressed shut, sunglasses straddling her head.

I caught a glimpse of them before the fog swallowed them up. They weren't just pigeons. There were little ones, too, the kind that hop around in puddles and pick at sand. And then something dark slid down the glass, a black clump of hair. Its tongue lolled, a pink curl. It was a cat. Someone was crying. Someone else was chanting "*ohmygodohmygodohmygod.*" I pictured the roof, several stories above us, filling up with birds and cats and squirrels and whatever other small, confused life was out there. Something let loose a strangled squawk. Ruth was crying like a Madonna, hands at her sides, palms up, crystal tears rolling down her soft, plump cheeks. Her hair had come loose and formed a halo of curls. Calle was gravitating toward the TV, even though Jason had shut it off. In a moment, I knew, she'd make a grab for the remote.

"Let's play a game!" someone shouted in a shaky voice full of forced enthusiasm. I rolled my eyes. Then I realized the voice belonged to me.

"A game? Are you serious?" Zosiah said.

"Let's go to the Game Room, then." Jason offered. Adrienne shot him a look.

"Yeah, why don't we go to my office and play a game?" Edison said.

"Are there any windows in there?" Ruth wondered aloud.

Edison shook his head. His hair was mussed. There were dark circles under his eyes.

We filed into Edison's office and stood in a clump by the door until he gestured toward the two chairs opposite his desk.

"Make yourselves at home."

I sat on the floor with my back against the wall while Edison rolled his chair out from behind his desk, then pushed the desk against the far wall to make room. The single picture frame fell over. Ruth picked it up.

"Is this your daughter?"

Edison nodded. He didn't look at the photo.

Ruth smiled down at the frame, gently set it back on the desk. "She's pretty. How old is she?"

"She's eight now." Edison sat down on the floor a few feet away from me, crossing his legs, his pants riding up to reveal worn-out dress socks. I looked around for Calle. She was sitting by the door, knees to her chest, rocking slightly. Ruth was whispering to Edison now. He shook his head.

"What game are we playing?" Zosiah nudged me with her bare foot. She was seated across from me, but the room was small enough she could extend a leg and touch me. I stiffened, then tried to force myself into a relaxed posture.

"Game?"

"Yeah, you said we should play a game." She had her purse in her lap. Her eyes shone, the irises too dark, too large. I bet her pupils were dilated.

"You can all play without me," Jason said. No one answered him.

Edison got up and fished around in his desk. He pulled out a mostly-full bottle of whiskey.

"This'll help us get started," he smiled.

They all clapped like he was a hero, except Calle. I imagined Edison taking nips of whiskey throughout the day while eyeing that photo of his daughter. Why hadn't he mentioned her when he introduced himself? She probably lived somewhere with her mother and Edison hardly ever saw her, just spoke to her on the phone once a week. *How are you, pumpkin? Fine. How is school? Fine. What do you want for your birthday? I dunno. . . .*

Now they were passing the bottle around, everyone taking a swig, even Calle, when prodded. Ruth had gone over to sit next to her and was rubbing her shoulders again. Calle looked ready to slap her.

"Let's play Truth or Dare," someone said.

"No, a drinking game. Never Have I Ever."

"Let's just drink."

I was thinking about my father, how he couldn't say he missed me so he put stickers advertising my alma mater all over his pristine car, how I always found cash in my pockets after a visit with him and yet never knew how he did it. I wanted my notebook, fumbled around for it in my bag. But when I found it, I just put it back. What was I going to do with it here, in front of everyone?

"I know, why don't we all say why we're here?" It was Edison. He had the bottle. Apparently he'd had a few turns with it already. He winked at me. "I know why this one's here." He grinned and clapped a hand on my shoulder.

"So do I," Zosiah said, smiling. She reached for the bottle, taking my turn, not that I minded.

"Why?" Ruth asked.

Zosiah took a swig. "Research."

I turned to her, surprised. What did she think I was researching?

Ruth nodded, accepting this answer without question. Edison wasn't listening.

"What about you?" Zosiah gestured with the bottle toward the two lovers. "Why are you two here?"

Ruth stiffened. Calle raised her head, glared at Zosiah. "Why do you think we're here?" She spat the words.

Zosiah looked away, passed the bottle on to Jason, who took it without a word, scowling as he wrapped his fist around the opening so his lips wouldn't touch the neck.

Calle covered her face with her hands and began to sob, silently. Jason got up, quickly lumbered toward her.

"Hey!" I cried as he reached up over her head and turned the light off. Suddenly all the room's edges were rubbed out. Adrienne moved her head and her glasses glinted. She had become a white, translucent outline of a person, a ghost with black hair floating around her head like tendrils of smoke. I couldn't stop looking at her.

"I'm being punished. God is punishing me for my sin."

Ruth leaned in, hair first, and tried to shh her but Calle shrugged her off.

"Well, I guess God is punishing all of us, then," Edison said. He didn't say, *I have a child, too.* Calle looked at him.

"I'm not judging you, or anyone," she snapped. "I'm only saying that I have sinned, sinned against my marriage."

Marriage? I looked at her hands. Sure enough, there was a simple band on her left ring finger. I tried to imagine what kind of man her husband might be. He was slight and smiled too big and too often. He had squinty blue eyes that saw without seeing.

Ruth stared at the floor. She looked smaller. She was leaning away from Calle now.

"Do you know how we met?" Calle went on.

"Stop," Ruth said quietly.

Calle jabbed her thumb at her. "She works at my son's school. His school." She paused, allowing this information to sink in.

I glanced at Zosiah, who was tapping her lower lip like she wasn't listening. Adrienne looked nonplussed. Ruth held her head up as tears filled her eyes and broke over her cheeks. Edison's expression had crumpled like a handful of tissues.

Calle shook her head. "God forgive me. I thought I was in love. God forgive me."

At that, Ruth got to her feet and slipped out of the room. Jason followed her. I followed Jason. She made it as far as the lobby, which was silent now. Jason had her by the shoulders and was whispering to her, close enough to kiss. Her eyes darted about.

"Hey," I said.

They both turned to me in surprise and then, just like that, the lights went out.

V

Ruth screamed. Someone gripped my arm hard, pulling on my sleeve. I heard footsteps thundering toward us and then with a "huh!" I hit the tile hard enough to knock the wind out of me and my soul with it. The pain was startling. I heard a scuffling, a wail, followed by grunts. The door shuddered in its frame; someone was trying to open it. I got to my feet.

"Ruth!" I cried, feeling around in the dark.

"Help!"

I heard shouts, shuffling, then rapid footsteps coming at us. A flare zoomed from one side of the room to the other, tracking flames across my field of vision.

"Hold on!" someone said.

The lights were back. I squinted, eyes tearing. I was facing the interior of the hotel. Before me was Edison, holding a flashlight, not a flare. Zosiah stood next to him, gripping his arm, Adrienne at her side, staring hard at me. No, not at me but something behind me. I heard a groan and turned to see Calle pressed against the door, Jason on top of her, pinning her arms behind her back, while Ruth looked on, hands over her mouth.

"What are you doing?" Edison pushed Jason out of the way. He wrapped his arm around Calle and led her to the couch.

"She was trying to get out! She's gonna get us all killed!"

"Calle," Edison put his hands on her shoulders, but she wouldn't meet his gaze. Her head turned, eyes roving like she was possessed. "Calle, it isn't safe to go out there. Okay? You need to stay in here."

Her eyes made their way to Edison's face, studied him for a moment. Then, with a roar, she jumped off the couch, knocking Edison off his feet, and rushed at the doors. Jason threw himself at her, wrapping his arms around her waist, and brought her down hard. He pressed her flat on her stomach and straddled her lower back as she struggled and groaned, pleading with him to let her go. We stood there, gaping.

Ruth and Adrienne started shouting. "You're hurting her!"

"Get off her!"

Jason glared at us. "I can't. If I get up, she's going for the door again."

"So let her." We all turned to Zosiah. She shrugged.

"Not an option," Jason said. Meanwhile, Calle lay flat on the floor, limbs splayed, panting.

"We can't open that door," Edison muttered as much to himself as to us. He looked at Jason. Something passed between them. Their faces hardened.

"Room 222?" Jason said. Only he wasn't asking, he was confirming.

Edison sighed. He nodded.

"No," Adrienne said with such urgency, it frightened me.

Jason climbed off Calle's back, then grabbed her by the arm and pulled her to her feet. Edison came forward to hold her other arm. They dragged her along toward the stairwell. Adrienne followed them, her hands balled into fists at her sides.

"Hey, where are you taking her?" Ruth raced after them.

"Stay here," Edison said.

Zosiah and I looked at each other. Then we took off running to catch up; they'd already reached the second floor and were heading into the hallway. Zosiah quickly got ahead of me, her purse jogging along, hitting her side. My legs were pumping but I felt weightless, hovering just above the floor.

"Wait!" I called, and she laughed as she went through the stairwell door, let it slam behind her. The muscles in my back burned as I flew up one flight, threw open the door and rushed into the hall, my heart pounding as I lengthened my stride, breathing double time. I almost slammed into Zosiah when I turned the corner and found them all in front of a room marked "222." Jason was holding Calle's arms behind her back. Edison opened the door. It was unlocked.

Black latex coated the floor. The walls were also black, a huge red orchid stenciled on the far wall opposite the door. A steel lamp with a slatted metal shade hung from a chain attached to the ceiling. Beneath it was a stretcher, padded like a mattress, with four cuff-like restraints hooked in: two for the wrists, two for the ankles. I stared at the stretcher. I was spinning. Already my back was aching and sore, the pain anchoring me to the flesh, holding me there, in the body. I couldn't climb out. Were they really doing this? Jason took hold of Calle's torso while Edison grabbed her legs.

"Wait," I said. No one seemed to hear me. I shouted. I turned to Ruth, who was watching the scene with her hands at her sides, mouth open, crying, "No."

"What the fuck, Jason?" It was Adrienne. Her face was flushed.

"It's for her own good." Jason began to lift her. As she rose off the floor, Calle bucked and kicked, hitting Edison in the jaw. He reeled backwards. Jason wrestled her to the floor. She was snarling, growling, spitting.

Zosiah moved in toward the stretcher, reached underneath to fiddle with some kind of lever, and the whole thing dropped down.

"C'mon," Jason glared, "I need everyone's help here."

Zosiah knelt on the floor in her bare feet, her leather skirt hitching up. Jason peered between her legs and grinned. I wanted to punch him. Or puke. Or puke on him.

"Wait. Wait, wait!" Ruth cried.

Adrienne grabbed my hand when Jason pinned Calle's arms down. Edison held her legs and Zosiah her waist as the three of them lifted her onto the stretcher, then fit the restraints around her wrists and ankles. In a moment, it was over. Gently, Zosiah raised the stretcher back up off the floor. Ruth was sobbing now.

Every visible inch of Calle's skin was scarlet. She tossed her head from side to side, strained and bucked against the braces. Finally, she went still. She was panting. "Ruth?" she said, very quietly. "Honey?"

Ruth shook her head and left the room.

"I have a son," Calle's voice broke. "I have a son." She said it over and over.

"You should rest now," Jason said and Calle went quiet.

"C'mon, guys," Edison herded us out. Already there was a shadow of a bruise forming on his jaw.

"You're just gonna leave her like that?"

"No, no." Edison held up his hands. He could hear me now. "Don't worry, we'll check on her, bring her food and water."

"Like a dog?"

"We did the right thing," Edison went on, ignoring me, searching the others' faces. "We couldn't let her go out there. Who knows what would happen to her?"

No one said, *And what will happen to us, in here?*

Adrienne shook her head. "You're fucking sick." She was looking at Jason.

"Hey," he blinked slowly. His lip drooped a little. He reached for her arm, but Adrienne recoiled.

"Don't touch me."

"Hey, hey," he said softly. Jason stepped in closer, his back to us, walling Adrienne off. He leaned in, whispering to her, and she rolled her eyes.

"You've gotta let her go," Ruth cried. Her hair had somehow grown into a copper crown. Tiny, shining coils framed her face. Her eyes were wet with tears, her lips swollen from crying. "You've gotta let her go." Ruth looked at us, one by one, pleading, landing on me last.

"We will, when it's safe," Edison patted her shoulder but she ignored him.

No one said anything more, Jason just went on whispering to Adrienne in the background till she sighed loudly and brushed him aside.

"I'm going to change," she addressed the group. "At my locker downstairs. Anyone want to come with me?" She looked past me, landed on Ruth and Zosiah.

My heart sank. If they all left, I'd be alone with Edison and Jason. Did they think that was where I belonged?

"You wanna look like a boy?" My mother scoffed. She couldn't stand my plain, loose uniform. It was my camouflage. She said I looked like I was always in pajamas. Then I cut my hair and she said, "Do you think you're a man?"

"No," I shot back, too fast to add anything about primitive binaries, about the balance of masculine and feminine, the space in between.

Her face fell. "*No?*" She was horrified. "Then what are you? Nothing?"

Nothing: an absence. A space awaiting fulfillment. Like a bowl or a womb—female. What was the opposite of nothing? *Everything.*

She shook her head. "I can't . . . I can't . . ." Her world was a mosaic of color-coded binaries, spaced in even intervals like the tiles on the bathroom floor.

"Try not to rile her up," my father always said, a warning not to tell her things she didn't want to hear.

Zosiah and Ruth said they were going back to the lobby. Adrienne headed down into the underbelly of the hotel, Edison returned to his office, perhaps to drink what was left of the whiskey, and Jason disappeared. I knew he was going to follow Adrienne but persuaded myself she could handle him, because there was nothing I could do then to stop him.

VI

I found Zosiah aiming the remote at the TV, angrily pressing buttons. The little light in the lower right corner told me the set was on, but the screen was blank.

"This fucking thing!" Zosiah threw the remote at the couch. It bounced off a cushion.

"The power's out," Ruth said quietly, as if whispering made the news less alarming.

Zosiah gestured to the lobby, the artificial light reflecting off the floors. "Then what's this?"

"Hotels have generators," I said. The two of them turned to look at me.

Ruth smiled. She had a way of looking directly into your eyes, her gaze unwavering, yet accepting of whatever it beheld. It felt good to be looked at like that.

"Zosiah and I were saying we should find the kitchen," she said. "Then we could bring Calle something." She forced her smile to widen while blinking back tears. It made sense that she worked with children. And yet there was a certain quiet power in her resolve. I studied her hair again. In this light, I could see the fine layer of red down on each side of her face, close to her ears.

I told them that was a good idea. We'd just wait for Adrienne to come back. Adrienne would know where the kitchen was, I reasoned, even though the hotel was relatively small, and I knew very well we could find the kitchen on our own. But no one pointed this out, so we just stood there, Ruth and I smiling at each other like professional acquaintances while Zosiah looked on. Behind them were the doors and windows, shrouded in cotton-polyester. I thought about whatever was seeping through those sheets, including the ones fitted under the door. My skin began to itch again. It's psychosomatic, I told myself. Still I wanted to get as far away from any kind of threshold as possible.

"Does your family live in the city?" Ruth asked me. She sat down on the couch, gestured for me to sit beside her.

"My parents are upstate."

Ruth nodded, "Mm hm." She kept on smiling at me. Calle hadn't said what Ruth did at her son's school. Maybe she was the counselor. *Do you have friends in your class? What do you like to do at recess?*

"What about you?"

"Oh, my family's in Vermont." Her face brightened. "My parents farm a little. And they make their own cheese and sell it at the summer markets. Vermont is so beautiful in the summer. It's beautiful in the winter, too, it's just your car gets stuck and you can't open the front door for all the snow sometimes." She laughed a short, hiccup-y laugh.

"Why did you leave then?" Zosiah sat down next to me, bumping me with her hip. She smiled at me in a way that said "sorry not sorry." She wanted my attention. I felt the heat of her next to me. She smelled like something earthy and spicy, like lemongrass or fennel, sweat, and faintly, leather.

"Not enough jobs. I came here with someone. But that ended. Then I found a job at the Heart's Day School."

"Heart's Day?" I echoed.

"No, Hearst Day."

"Oh."

"That's in Westchester," Zosiah said with a sudden accent that seemed more accidental than affected. She brushed a strand of hair out of her face, and I saw it again, that streak of white, a little lightning in her hair. *I like my women with lightning in their hair.* My father said a woman's hair was "everything" and smiled wistfully after long manes and generous pony tails. But my mother hadn't worn her hair long since before I was born.

When I cut mine, he nodded in approval.

"Very fine."

"Yes, that's right." Ruth nodded at Zosiah. Then she paused, looked down at her hands in her lap, her fingers knitted together. "I'm supposed to be at work right now. I took the day off to be with Calle. If I hadn't done that, I'd be with her son right now." She tried to smile but began to cry instead. Tears were certainly warranted, though I could see that she cried easily. My mother would've shaken her head in disapproval.

My mother grew giant, bitter vegetables that no one wanted to eat, just because she'd always grown them and refused to trade them in for flowers. It was decadent, she said, to forgo sustenance for vanity. I think she just liked having rules to follow. And one of her rules was that women should never get hysterical, or do anything to suggest they might become hysterical, despite her own breakdowns.

There was never a name for what she had. At least, none was offered. She was simply my mother who mostly behaved like one person, until another, less practical mother took over, one who failed to follow schedules or notice dust or a dying plant or hungry children. That was all.

Yet, as a teen, she wore black and wrote short, block paragraphs of bad poetry. She never told me; I was snooping through her drawers one day, getting my mitts all over her shiny, synthetic nightgowns with square, lace collars and flouncy sleeves, neat rows of paired socks. Underneath, I found a polaroid of a girl in tight black jeans sneering at the camera while holding a beer, fingers stained with ink, an arm belonging to someone out of frame slung over her shoulder. Her painted nails were chipped. Who was this girl? There was a poem on the back that I didn't understand. It included the words "cock" and "la petite mort." My mother never spoke French, or employed French phrases. The Jane I knew applied her poetic talent to the custom greeting cards she sold online. She made enough to take my father on a cruise but still called it a hobby. She worried the hem of her sweater when she was nervous.

I studied that photo of young Jane and imagined a whole other life for her, one where she smoked cigarettes and wrote poetry all night and had a daughter like she'd always wanted to resent and coax into womanhood. I imagined a life for her in which I did not exist.

I thought of Calle lying there in room 222, strapped down like Bertha in some S&M version of *Jane Eyre*, crying for her child. I replayed her confession in Edison's office, how she had "thought" she was in love. An overwhelming pity for Ruth washed over me and carried me up and out of my seat. She and Zosiah gazed up at me.

Ruth wiped at her eyes with her shirtsleeve. "I'm sorry," she said. "This is just . . ." She trailed off. "You know, when I was little, I believed in angels?" She smiled. "And fairies, too. I believed they were all around us, in the air, protecting us." Her smile fell. "But then someone told me, if angels are everywhere, then so are devils." Her voice dropped a half step. "So I stopped believing."

"Do you believe in God?" She looked at me with such earnestness. There was nothing I could say in response that wouldn't disappoint her.

"I believe in stories," I offered.

Adrienne reappeared wearing ripped jeans and a T-shirt, her hair in a loose topknot. She seemed much younger than she'd appeared in her uniform, yet even hipper. How old was she, really? Even if no one under eighteen could ever get a job at the hotel, that still made her little more than a teenager, though we were probably only a handful of years apart. Which meant I myself was also just a kid. But it didn't feel that way. I felt like the longtime custodian of this body, charged with caring for it like an antique piece of furniture.

I expected Jason to come sliding around the corner in his ridiculous coveralls, a smug grin on his face. He'd be the only one left in uniform now, unless you counted Edison's suit. Ruth sniffled, said something kind to Adrienne about her clothes. In response, Adrienne shrugged.

I held my breath, still waiting for Jason, but he failed to appear. Then Zosiah piped up, told Adrienne we were all starving and would she please take us to the kitchen to get something to eat?

"We'll pay for it, of course," Ruth said.

Zosiah shot her a look.

"I don't think you're going to have to worry about that," Adrienne said. "C'mon. Follow me."

The kitchen was a huge rectangle of a room with counters lining the two longer walls, bookended by giant ovens and stoves, an island prep station in the middle, spongy rubber mats covering the floor to collect dropped foodstuff. I'd worked at a restaurant one summer in high school, and though I got fired after a couple weeks, I remembered they had similar mats on the floor which someone had to hose down outside near the dumpsters at the end of the day to flush out all the mushed-up wet crumbs and vegetable ends, bits of meat and fat and other disgustingness. But there hadn't been time for this floor mat to get much use that day, so it was still relatively clean.

Adrienne gave us a tour, showing off the walk-in freezer and giant pantry full of rice, potatoes, flour, canned goods, and other staples. She grabbed a piece of fruit from a bin and tossed it to me.

"Here."

It was an unripe persimmon, golden orange, with a fringe of green on top.

"They're my favorite," she said.

"Thanks."

Overhead, the fluorescent lights buzzed and flickered. How long would the generator last? Didn't those things run out of juice eventually?

Meanwhile, Zosiah had taken it upon herself to scope out the giant fridge. "Ooh!" she called, "they have good cheese in here!" She poked her head out from behind the fridge's silver door. "Is there wine, too?"

"Are there eggs in there?" asked Ruth.

"Yeah, of course."

"I could really go for an omelet." She turned to me. "What about you?"

I forced a smile, then shrugged. I hadn't had breakfast, but I didn't have much of an appetite yet.

Zosiah started pulling things out of the fridge and setting them on the island, first one at a time, then double-fisting: a carton of duck eggs, bricks of cheese, pickles, pickled beets, gourmet apple sauce, rainbow carrots. "There's cake in here!" A jar of maraschino cherries, containers of fresh berries, muffins, pasta salad, chicken salad, tuna salad, smoked trout, and hunks of shrink-wrapped raw meat and fish piled up on the counter.

"Where are the utensils? Does anyone else want an omelet?"

I told Ruth I would have one.

Zosiah picked up a fork and speared a hunk of chocolate cake right out of the container.

"There's pie, too," Adrienne said, and Zosiah's eyes bulged. She hopped up and down, then went back to the fridge to dig for the pie.

Her frenzy was contagious. With my finger, I scooped up a whip of chocolate frosting and took a tentative lick. Zosiah set a berry galette down on the counter and grinned. Then she took her phone out of her purse. I thought she was going to take a picture of the food, which seemed a little odd under the circumstances, but instead music started to flow out of the phone's tiny speaker. For a moment, it unnerved me. I'd gotten used to the quiet of the hotel, and now a singer's cherry-soda-pop voice was filling the room with bubbles, the kitchen's acoustics magnifying the sound, the lights blinking like a cheap club full of underage girls. A fork in one hand, her mouth full of cake, Zosiah began to dance about the room, doing a sexy shuffle-like boogie. I thought of ghost ship legends, of wealthy passengers waltzing the night away on a doomed vessel, spiraling down into the frigid depths. Ruth was clapping her hands, bobbing her head a little, rocking side to side while Adrienne looked on.

"That music sucks," she said.

"Here," Zosiah tossed the phone to Adrienne. "Put on something else then."

She shook her head, set the phone down on the island. "Nah, I don't care enough to ruin it for you."

Zosiah sidled up to her, ground her ass against Adrienne's hip, working her magic till Adrienne smirked and then suddenly both of them were laughing hysterically, dark grains of cake stuck in the crevices between Zosiah's teeth.

"I'm making omelets!" Ruth cried again, now standing in front of the stove, heating a pan, a bowl of beaten duck eggs on the counter beside her. "With real eggs!" No one answered her.

I scanned the shelves for a plate I could put a piece of pie on.

"Just eat!" Zosiah cried, bumping my hip with hers. I felt myself flush. Without thinking, I dug my hand into the pie. Zosiah laughed.

Suddenly, we were feasting frantically, gnawing on hunks of cheese, dipping carrot slices in Ranch dressing, stuffing our mouths with various meats and berries and cake, plus the omelets Ruth made for all of us, which were light and fluffy, with shredded spinach, the cheese gooey and salty. We munched on croutons and crackers and sardines, devoured a box of jelly donuts someone found stashed in a cabinet, washing it all down with a nice Malbec Zosiah uncorked. We passed it around, pressing our lips to it one after the other, the neck sticky and slick from our dirty, jelly-covered fingers, while the music beat on, its optimism undeterred by the giant, menacing cloud advancing on the city. Delirious, full to bursting, I took another dive into the pie and Adrienne picked it up, offering me the whole thing, then pressed my face into it, laughing. I threw a fistful of berries at her, but she ducked, and they splattered like viscera on the floor. Zosiah rubbed her legs and feet down with olive oil. She slid across the floor, trailed by glistening snail streaks. Was the same pop song just playing over and over? We ate and ate till Ruth threw up in the sink, holding her own hair back. Then we were thirsty. Ruth washed away the puke, and we drank cold water straight from the tap. It ran down our shirtfronts, blotting the stains.

By the end, we were sleepy and swollen, lying half curled up on the floor, or atop the steel counters. Zosiah drained the last drop of wine, knocked the bottle on its side, and let it spin.

"Let's play Spin the Bottle," she said and laughed. She gave it a turn. It landed on no one.

"Come closer," she called to us, and we drew toward her as if compelled, past the fridge, close to the door, where the mat stopped and the cold tile began, our eyes heavy, faces smeared with various delicacies. Adrienne lay down in a half-assed yoga pose, her back flat against the floor. Zosiah spun again. This time the bottle selected Ruth. She giggled, shook her head. No, no. She wouldn't play. Zosiah crawled toward her on her hands and knees, planted a three-second kiss (I counted) hard on her mouth. They all laughed.

"Now you spin."

Ruth landed on the pantry.

"Closer, closer," Zosiah gestured for us to move in, tighten up the circle. Her eyes were half-closed. She had probably gotten the lion's share of the wine. Well, why not? There were more bottles, enough for us to each have one, to have several if we wanted. Adrienne probably wasn't of age. But what did it matter?

Ruth spun again. She got me. Adrienne and Zosiah whooped and hollered. I sat there, a smile frozen on my face, my heart racing. Now she had to touch me, but she wouldn't want to. Ruth began scooching her way toward me, smiling sheepishly as she went. I realized she was actually going to kiss me, though her lover was a few floors above us, strapped down on a sex stretcher, because she was that kind of nice; she wouldn't want to hurt my feelings by denying me physical contact, as if she owed me that.

"You don't have to . . ." I sputtered.

We were nose to nose, her hair enveloping us both. She smelled of roses and earth. Before I even had time to close my eyes, Ruth kissed me softly and suddenly I saw myself at thirteen, my first real middle school party, how the bottle had swung around wildly, the kids shouting and crowing, shoving into a closet the couples they paired so easily, boy-girl, boy-girl, while I hid in the stairwell, sipping fruit punch to calm myself, shaking, red-faced, and confused.

In an instant, it was over. Zosiah and Adrienne applauded the effort half-heartedly.

"Well done. Now my turn." Zosiah slunk toward me like a hunter, grinning as she went. Paralyzed, I watched her approach. She swiped at the bottle, knocking it out of the way. It rolled off, clinking against the tile. Now she mashed her lips against mine, and I tasted the rich meld of our feast, the chocolate notes and acid from the alcohol, pickle brine and cheese funk. Her tongue emerged, a little snail darting here and there, testing and tasting. This time, I remembered to close my eyes. I felt a crackling rush, fizz in my blood.

When she finished, the others did not clap.

The music had shut off. Or maybe I just couldn't hear it anymore.

"Well," Ruth began, but that was all she said.

We sat there with a silence blossoming, its petals lolling like tongues, reaching to touch with their pointed tips the spaces between us, and with it came the sudden strain of remembering that we were, in fact, strangers. Tipsy, overfed strangers covered in food in a hotel kitchen we had trashed. I surveyed the damage, which made it easier to avoid my companions' eyes.

The counters were covered in open containers and ripped bags of food. There were crushed berries, chocolate smears. Raw egg was dripping onto the floor. The food-trap mat surely needed to be washed out. Who would do it? Adrienne? I risked a quick glance at her. She was staring at the floor, her head tilted to one side, baring the graceful slope of her young neck. Her topknot accentuated her teacup ears, curving outward as if they didn't want to miss anything. I decided that if she started to clean up, so would I, even though all kinds of machinations and gases were setting to work in my gut, mumbling and squeezing and groaning, so movement seemed impossible. Yet, at the same time, I wanted very badly to get far away from that room. I did not belong here, I didn't fit. I was supposed to be at a cafe where the baristas probably knew me by sight but never let on because I bought too little for the hours I spent there, or maybe they just didn't care, wishing they also had somewhere better to be. It was either that, tucked in a corner at a sticky table almost too small to accommodate my laptop and coffee and notebook, or back in the apartment, behind my shower-curtain partition, my bed serving as my workspace while my roommates were off at their offices.

Right now, my mother was probably sitting in front of that old TV set in the kitchen, watching the news and twisting the hem of the sweater she wore all year round, her hands smelling of the garlic and onions she'd chopped for dinner the night before. She'd stare intently at the screen as if they might quickly pan to my face, and if she blinked, she'd miss it. In the background, my father was on the phone, his voice friendly to disguise his panic as he tried to reach someone at some government office.

He'd probably called the local police already and spoken to the town sheriff, to whom my Jewish mother sent a knitted hat every year for Christmas.

I patted my chest, searching for the strap of my messenger bag. It wasn't there. I remembered taking the bag off in Edison's office. I had to recover my notebook. Without it, I couldn't hold onto any of this, let alone the world outside this place. I prepared myself to stand up but before I made the attempt, Ruth rose gracefully to her feet. We all looked up at her in surprise.

"I should bring Calle something," she said, surveying the kitchen like she didn't know where to begin.

"You wanna make her an omelet?" Zosiah offered.

Ruth nodded, "That's a good idea." Amidst the mess, she set about beating the eggs and chopping the spinach all over again, while the rest of us sat on the floor and watched. This time she moved haltingly, second-guessing herself. There wasn't enough space on the countertops and the bowl of beaten eggs spilled onto the mats.

"Oh no." Ruth sank to her knees, staring at the bowl where the egg had been. "Oh no."

No one moved to help her. It had become clear that we wouldn't be cleaning up the mess at all.

Ruth studied the bowl, then the floor, then the empty bowl again. She sighed, began moving more mess from the counter into the sink. She beat the remaining eggs vigorously, for longer than was necessary. No one made a peep while she cooked, not even when she expertly flipped the omelet in the pan.

When she was finished, she set the omelet on a plate and garnished it with the remaining fruit. Adrienne brought her a room-service tray, and together we made our way back upstairs.

We agreed to wait for Ruth in the lobby. The silence there was unsettling. I needed to find my bag but I didn't want to break away from the group to go searching for it.

After a few minutes, Ruth emerged from the hallway, the tray still laden with food.

"What happened?" we asked.

Her eyes darted about. "The door's locked."

We made our way to Edison's office where we found him at his desk, leaning so far back in his chair it looked like he was about to fall over. I thought he might be asleep, but he was studying the ceiling. Jason was sitting on the floor, my messenger bag next to him. I grabbed it and slung it over my shoulder, quickly checked inside for my notebook.

"Edison, we need the key to 222," Adrienne said.

He sat up, tipping forward. "Oh. What? 222? Why?"

Adrienne gestured toward the tray in Ruth's arms.

"I see." He looked us over.

"What have you all been up to?" Jason chided. No one answered.

Edison opened his desk drawer, took out a tiny key, then unlocked a second drawer with it. "Hold on," he said, rummaging around. Keys jangled.

"I have it," Jason said.

"Oh, well, there you go." Edison nodded.

"I'll take her the food." Jason climbed to his feet. Zosiah and Adrienne exchanged glances as Jason raised his arms up over his head in a stretch, looming over us, his fingers grazing the ceiling.

"No, I want to bring it to her," Ruth said.

"I don't think that's a good idea."

"C'mon," Adrienne said, "give her the key."

Jason shook his head. "No can do."

"Fine," Adrienne sighed, "I'll just get the key from my desk."

Jason grinned. "Got that one, too."

"From my desk?"

"Jason, just give her the key," Edison cut in. He was rubbing his eyes, which were bloodshot, the skin underneath turning purplish to match the bruise on his jaw, where Calle had kicked him.

"All right, all right," Jason held up his hands in surrender. He fished around in his pocket for a while, finally pulling out a brass key with "222" on its head. Adrienne snatched it out of his hand.

"I'll take her." She and Ruth left the office. Zosiah and I turned to follow.

"You're all going?" Edison sounded disappointed.

Zosiah and I looked at each other. "We're just going to the lobby," she said.

"Oh," Edison brightened. "I'll join you." He got up slowly, holding onto the desk to steady himself. I had a feeling the whiskey he'd shared before wasn't his only bottle. We made our way back to the exact spot I didn't want to be in, with Jason following along, whistling loudly to himself.

A few minutes later, Ruth reappeared, with Adrienne following close behind her, frowning. Ruth was holding the tray, the omelet still intact, oozing rubbery cheese.

"She didn't want it." Her voice was soft. She bowed her head.

"What did she say?" Zosiah asked.

Ruth didn't look up.

I glanced at Adrienne. She shrugged. "I didn't go in with her."

"Told you," Jason said.

Ruth began to cry.

"Gimme the tray," Jason reached for it. "I'll give it to her."

"No," Ruth turned away sharply. A tear fell on the omelet. "No," I added.

"I think we all need a minute," Zosiah said. Her eyes were red. Everyone fell quiet. Jason clenched his teeth.

Edison gently took the tray from Ruth, then sat down and began eating the cold eggs.

"I know a spot." Adrienne went over to the front desk and quickly removed a key.

She was right; we needed to get out of here.

"We're all going?" Edison looked up. He sounded hopeful yet there was a note of fear in his voice.

No one answered.

"Yeah, can't we go with you lovely ladies?" Jason cried, holding his arms out like he expected a hug. I stepped back and caught his eye. "You, too," he said, daring me to say something, start something. I scowled, my pulse thrumming, and he winked. I imagined him crushing me in a bear hug, how he'd laugh harder and harder while I struggled as he slowly squeezed me like bellows, compressing the air out of me. "Whatsamatter? It's just a hug," he'd say. "Boys will be boys," my mother said, apropos of nothing.

I waited to see if he'd follow us but to my relief Jason stayed put as we quickly filed out of the lobby, skipped the elevator, and headed for the stairs to climb the four flights to room 406.

VII

The door opened to reveal a spacious room laden with Persian rugs and dozens of plush, saffron pillows topping the fainting couches—out of place, considering the motif—upholstered in teal, yellow, and pink silk. A large window was shaded by metal latticework inlaid with jewels. Pastel drawings of belly dancers decorated the walls.

"This is the Harem Room," Adrienne shrugged. "It's one of the few that's big enough for all of us."

I went over to the window. The fog outside made the glass appear translucent, like staring into the cloudy nebula within a crystal ball. The little hairs on the back of my neck stood up. I retreated, chose a spot closer to the door.

Zosiah and Adrienne started fashioning beds out of pillows while Ruth sat against the wall, close to the window. She left the pillows and couches alone. I asked her if she was comfortable, and she nodded, smiling weakly.

I awoke to total darkness and for a moment, I was still in a nightmare. A man in a stuffy little fish tank of an office was watching a checkerboard of hotel rooms on a screen, like God's own peep show. All night he observed unsuspecting strangers as they wept soundlessly, gorged themselves on snacks, consuming their own tears, even their sodden tissues. They tore their clothes, cut their hair, ripped the stuffing out of the pillows.

Then, someone sighed, gently. The sound was familiar, grounding. I was there in the hotel, awake. My leg twitched of its own accord. *Let go,* I told my body. *Release.* I managed to sit up and rubbed at my eyes, as if that would help me see. The inside of my mouth tasted foul and my teeth were scuzzy. I scanned the soft humps of bodies and pillows scattered about the room. Something was piled against the wall by the window. It was Ruth, I realized. It was her sigh I'd heard. She wasn't moving but I could tell she was awake. It was too dark to find my notebook, let alone write it in, not that I hadn't tried scribbling in the dark before. My notebook sat on the windowsill by my bed every night. Sometimes ideas surfaced while I slept and became indecipherable scrawls for me to puzzle over in the morning.

I stood up and felt my way toward Ruth, feet shuffling around. My knee bumped a couch and I apologized to it. Someone sighed, rolled over, the sound like the rustling of taffeta petticoats. I paused, waiting. The room went quiet again.

By the time I got there, my eyes had adjusted to the dark. I crouched down in front of Ruth.

"Hey," I whispered.

She smiled at me, mouthed "Hello," then put a finger to her lips.

I pressed my hands together, held them to the side of my face, and tilted my head. A question: *Can't sleep?*

Ruth shook her head.

I didn't know what I could mime in response, so I stuck out my lower lip as far as it would go. She nodded. Then I held out my hand to her, palm up, reaching close so she could see it. Ruth paused a moment before she took it. Her skin was dry and cold, her grip firm. I recalled our kiss in the kitchen, her soft, moist mouth, and my face flushed.

In the palm of my hand, she scratched messages I couldn't make out, though I caught a heart and a "you." I didn't think I was that "you." Her fingers moved faster and faster, and as they went, tears rolled down her cheeks, slid off her jaw and into the dark. Ruth smiled as she cried, though it wasn't really a smile anymore, but a grimace. I wanted to know the story she was telling, and yet I felt in some way that I already did.

After a while, Ruth removed her hand and wiped at her face. She stopped crying. Neither of us spoke or mimed another message. I closed my eyes and let my body dissolve. There was no room, no hotel walls. I might've fallen asleep again.

A rustling sound brought me back, followed by a stifled mew. Someone else was having a nightmare. I peered into the black. There was thrashing, a moan. Then silence. I tried to make my body bleed away again, but I couldn't do it.

Somebody got up. I saw a shadow heading for the door. All of a sudden, the lights came on. I squinted, the room so bright my eyes teared. Someone else groaned.

"What the fuck?" Zosiah said.

"Sorry." Adrienne stood by the light switch, her hair undone, loose, messy waves falling over her shoulders. Her glasses were on but the eyes behind them were bloodshot. "I set a timer on my phone." She held it up for us to see.

Zosiah glared at her as she stood up to stretch. She'd taken her skirt off and her blouse just barely covered her hips. I turned away, pretending to examine a framed, gold-leaf print on the wall of a naked woman dancing with scarves. I wondered if that room I'd found her in, the Garden Room with the nest for a bed, was still unlocked.

I let the others use the bathroom first. Meanwhile, I drifted back to the window and peered through the ornate latticework to take another peek at the outside world.

The view had changed. Or maybe it was just that my view of *it* had changed. The fog seemed uniform now, almost solid, like gray sheets of insulation pressed flat against the glass. I sucked in my breath, closed my eyes. It would swallow cars, fill the lungs. With what? Nothing. The city was gone, drowned. The walls of this building had become the limits of the world. I felt dizzy, I was sweating, my jaw clenched. My parents were at home among the trees in their A-frame house with a detached garage that was always open. Behind me, two people were talking. Their voices were getting louder, the pitch higher.

I turned to them. "What's going on?"

Adrienne had her arms crossed over her chest. Chin down, she peered at me over the rim of her glasses. "She says she's going up to the roof."

"The roof?"

Ruth was composed, her posture relaxed. Her eyes were dry, though bloodshot. I saw her sitting by the window again, awake in the dark.

"Wait, what? She's going where?" Zosiah came out of the bathroom, her skirt back on.

"I'm going to go up there and see if I can flag down a helicopter," she said, enunciating each word like a vow.

"A helicopter?" I repeated. There were no helicopters. I hadn't heard a single one. It had been hours since I'd even heard a siren, a realization that was not exactly comforting. I waited for someone to say something more, to explain to Ruth that there was nothing to flag down. That she wouldn't be seen, even if there had been. But no one said anything. No one wanted to be the one to do it, to speak the unspeakable: no one was coming for us. There was no rescue to await: the hotel *was* the rescue.

"You can't open the door!" Zosiah cried.

Ruth glanced at Adrienne.

"What?" Zosiah said.

Adrienne scratched her neck. "Well, there's a series of doors leading up to the roof. If you closed one after the other, technically, you could go up there without breaking the seal."

Zosiah gaped at Adrienne, who meanwhile studied the floor, grimacing, her hands on her hips. She had dark circles under her eyes now, in addition to the redness.

Ruth was patiently waiting for one of us to say more, but we just stood there, stricken. I combed my hair with my fingers, returning to the Sisyphean task of smoothing down my cowlick.

"Adrienne," Ruth said softly, "show me how to get to the roof."

She shook her head.

"That's all right." Ruth smiled as if Adrienne had confessed to not knowing the way.

Adrienne started chewing her lip. Her nostrils flared and her glasses misted up. Zosiah was flushed and clutching her purse. Her expression reminded me of the moment she'd looked outside, down in the lobby, and seen the descending cloud for the first time. I recalled how she'd turned back to the room, wearing a different face. I shuddered.

"I think you've lost your mind," Zosiah said sharply. She pointed at Ruth. *J'accuse.*

Ruth gave her a sympathetic nod but said nothing, which only seemed to further irritate Zosiah. She looked to Adrienne, then at me, eyes wide.

"You're all crazy," she said, scowling at Adrienne.

"What do you want us to do, tie her up?" Adrienne removed her glasses to wipe at the lenses with her shirt.

Zosiah glared at her. Then she sniffled and wiped her face with the back of her hand, releasing her purse for a moment. "Why not? Is that any worse than letting her do this?"

I knew she was going, no matter what we said, because no one would physically hold her back. I thought about how we'd held hands in the dark, the story she'd written on my palm. If we couldn't stop her, we could at least go with her.

"It's all right," Ruth said, as if she could hear me. "Just show me where to go. Who knows what I might be able to see from up there?"

Calle was still two floors below us, strapped to a bed. Had anyone given her water? My bladder reminded me it was my turn to use the restroom. Had anyone gone to help her? "Anyone" would have to mean Jason. We had to go back down there. That was the move. And Ruth wasn't coming with us.

Whatever had happened between them, whatever this had done to them, it had reached a point of no return. So we'd attend to Ruth now, then Calle.

"All right," Adrienne's voice came out hoarse, like she'd been screaming and screaming. She put her glasses back on. "I'll show you the staircase. Close each door behind you."

Ruth smiled. "Thank you."

Zosiah was shaking her head. "This is insane. We can't just let her . . . She's going to let in . . ."

Ruth moved in closer and set a hand on Zosiah's arm. "I'll be careful." Her countenance was starting to remind me of death. Not real-life death, of which I'd seen only glimpses, but made-for-TV-movie death, where a character was lucid and noble, resigned to their doom, a shitty fate no one in real life would ever have been okay with. For a moment, I was furious. I'd been cheated by a bad performance. What was Ruth trying to pull? Was the saintly demeanor all an act? Did she have a plan of escape that she could only execute alone?

I met Ruth's gaze for a moment and her expression of unwavering acceptance and resolve told me to let go. Instead, the loss welled up. I was very tired. I fervently hoped she was leaving us all behind to save herself and her lover. I imagined her putting on a gas mask, leaping off the roof, tethered by a rope that had somehow been there all along. She'd swing through a giant window I knew didn't exist. Then she'd rescue Calle.

I saw her lying on top of dead pigeons, gasping, writhing. I saw her face turn blue-black, then disappear into the fog. But it was her choice.

"We're all going with you," I said.

"I can't believe you're going along with this," Zosiah hissed.

My face went hot. "It's her decision to make."

Zosiah pressed her lips together in a tight line. She didn't say anything more, just shook her head and glared.

VIII

We processed slowly through the maze of the hotel, Adrienne leading the way, the rest of us walking side by side in a row of three. Together, we formed a triangle. Ruth held her head up, arms loose at her sides. Eventually, we reached the stairwell. The light was dim. As we made our way toward the top of the building, the only sounds were our labored breaths, accompanied by the dull, thudding rhythm of our footsteps.

At last, we reached the tenth floor. Adrienne slowly opened the door into the hall, looked both ways before leading us through. We padded across carpet soft as moss, following her turn after turn, passing rooms with the same sleek, poker-faced doors, the numbers shining in gold. Finally, we reached a small door, the same color as the walls, invisible, except for the steel handle.

"There's another stairway through here," Adrienne said. "Go up, and at the top, you'll find a door, then another door to the roof. But you can only open it from this side. Once it closes, you can't get back in."

Ruth nodded. "Thank you."

"So, just remember, the door . . ."

Ruth nodded again, cut her off. "I know."

We all stood there not knowing what to do, till finally Ruth embraced us, one at a time. "Thank you," she whispered to me, and my heart seized.

We hung back in a cluster, watched as she opened the door. I held my breath.

She smiled brightly. "See you soon."

Adrienne looked away, stuck her hands in her pockets. Zosiah was pale. Her hair hung over her shoulders, suddenly shaggy, all its luster gone, the strand of white grazing her cheek.

Ruth opened the door and passed into the stairwell. The door closed behind her.

*

We waited for something to happen. I listened for footsteps, but there were none. She had disappeared. Or else the heavy door muffled the sound. I heard a sigh, turned to see Zosiah sliding down against the wall to the floor, hands covering her face, shoulders spasming. I willed my body to say something, do something, go sit beside her and put my arm around her, but it wouldn't move.

"I've had enough of this game," Zosiah said to no one in particular, to the hotel itself.

Enough is enough is enough, I thought. "We have to go check on Calle."

Adrienne blinked at me. "Yeah," she said slowly. "Okay. You're right."

"Go without me." Zosiah waved us away, her chin tucked against her chest. Her hair hid her face.

"Nope." The volume of my voice surprised me.

"You can't stay here alone," Adrienne chimed in.

"Fuck you. Fuck this place." Zosiah dismissed us with another wave.

"You can walk or we'll carry you, but you aren't staying here." Adrienne was the youngest of us, and yet she was holding it together better than anyone. Or, at least, that's how it seemed to me. I'd started shaking and I couldn't stop.

"I'm not going, I'm staying right here!" Zosiah screamed like a child.

"How are we gonna carry her?"

Adrienne shrugged. "You take her head, I'll take her feet." I thought of Calle again, how Edison and Jason had carried her like a rolled-up carpet. How Jason had held her down. How Zosiah had helped them. How I'd let it happen. It was all over in a moment.

Zosiah looked up at us, incredulous. She climbed to her feet. "No."

"All right then," Adrienne said.

The three of us headed back to the stairs.

IX

When we reached room 222, we stood outside the door for a moment, listening. Nothing. Then, a quick, hollow jingle, like the rattling of a bicycle chain, followed by silence.

Adrienne pulled the brass key out of her pocket and opened the door.

It was dark inside and smelled of urine.

"Calle?" she called.

I felt along the wall for the light switch. Someone else found it first. In the blink of an eye, the whole room lit up, bright as an OR.

Zosiah gasped. Calle lay on the stretcher, her whole body flushed and puffy, slick with a sheen of sweat, her wrists and ankles rubbed raw from the restraints. Her eyes were closed, her mouth hung open.

"Oh my God, is she . . . ?" Gripping her purse, Zosiah peered down at Calle, then leaned in close, her ear nearly touching her lips. She smiled with relief. "She's breathing."

Calle groaned. Her head snapped forward as her whole body convulsed. Zosiah screamed. The stretcher shook as she bucked against the restraints. Her jaw clamped shut. I was afraid she'd bite her tongue.

Suddenly, she stopped. She was panting. I took a tentative step forward. Her eyes were open.

"Calle." I heard Adrienne's slow, even voice behind me. "We came to check on you."

Her eyes fixed on Adrienne. She didn't blink.

Adrienne started backing out of the room, motioned for us to follow her.

"We obviously can't let her go," Zosiah whispered.

I didn't want to admit that she was probably right. Something was clearly wrong with Calle, but letting her loose wouldn't help. What would, then? I scratched my neck, then my arm, before I stopped myself. Adrienne was watching me.

"We can't leave her like that," I said.

"What other choice do we have? Did you see her?" Zosiah pointed at the door.

"It's not safe." I wondered if Adrienne meant for Calle, or for us.

"What if we untie her, but we lock her in?" I offered, though I worried she could still hurt herself, alone in the room.

"Can't you open the door from the inside?"

"Not without a key," Adrienne said.

We traded glances.

Zosiah said, "Okay, but who's going to do it?"

"It has to be quick. Get it done, then right out of the room."

"I'll do it," Adrienne offered.

"No, you have to stay outside with the key." Zosiah sighed. "I'll do it." She turned to me. "You should stay by the wall and cut the lights as soon as I'm done."

"What? Why?"

"So she can't grab me."

"But how will you find your way out?"

"I've been in and out of that room a couple times. If I'm already moving when you get the lights, I should make it. It's not that far." She seemed sure of herself.

Adrienne and I looked at each other. She shrugged. "Okay," I said.

I went in first, treading carefully, as if the floor might cave in. Zosiah followed me. I got into position, and she slipped past me. I couldn't tell if Calle's eyes were open. Her face was so swollen, her features were misshapen. Slowly, her chest rose and fell. Zosiah began undoing the restraints at her feet. The charm on her bracelet trembled as she moved.

"Don't kick me, now," she said, forcing a laugh.

Calle did not so much as twitch as Zosiah started in on her wrists. Her hair had fallen over her face and hung down, brushing Calle's shirt. Suddenly, Zosiah turned, extending her limbs, ready to run.

"Now!"

I hit the light switch and when the room disappeared, I stayed where I was, waiting for Zosiah to pass me by. I heard a shuffle, then a crash. I turned the lights back on. Zosiah was lying on the floor and Calle remained on the stretcher. Adrienne rushed in behind me. Together, we helped Zosiah to her feet. Her knee was scraped.

"I'm fine. I tripped." She brushed us off and walked past us, limping slightly. Her fall reminded me of my own bruised back, which began to ache again.

We followed Zosiah out of the room, and Adrienne locked the door. I winced when the key turned, expecting a bang or a howl, but there was nothing, which was almost worse. A wave swept over me, lifted me up and then set me down like a rag doll, doubled over. Calle was gone. We'd locked someone away but it was not Calle. And Ruth had left us. *It was her choice, I didn't stop her this time.* I gasped for breath, then forced myself upright. Panting, I looked around.

Adrienne was watching me. "You okay?"

I shook my head. Then froze. "What if Jason comes back?"

Zosiah was leaning against the wall. She rubbed her hip like it was sore. "So what?"

"He won't come back." Adrienne sounded sure of herself.

"How do you know?" I asked.

"He won't," she snapped. "He'll just leave her there."

I hoped she was right.

*

We traveled back to the lobby like a beast with six legs, shoulders rubbing as we peeked around each corner. We all understood without saying it that we couldn't be seen near Calle's room. *Calle's room.* I cringed. Calle's cell was more like it.

We were about to enter the lobby when we heard a loud thump. We froze, eyes wide, hands up, muscles tensed. Then we heard it again, followed by a bumping-shudder sound. I looked at Adrienne. She looked at Zosiah, who pointed at Edison's door, only a few yards away. Then she took a step back toward the stairs, motioning for us to follow.

Right then, Jason burst out of the office. He headed straight for the lobby, swearing to himself as he went.

Did he see us? Zosiah mouthed.

I shook my head.

We crept up to the door, and I peered in. The office was empty. Not just of people, but furniture, too. What had he been doing in there?

I moved past the office into the lobby. Adrienne followed close behind but Zosiah hung back. Adrienne motioned impatiently for her to follow. She shook her head. We kept on without her. Then I heard her trotting after us.

I found the white couches pressed up against the doors, along with Edison's desk and an assortment of chairs and plant stands, forming a barricade. A chain tied the door handles together. Orchids were still strewn about and the floor was littered with petals, chips of marble, dried out tangles of moss. Torn and wrinkled papers lay on the floor, complementing a haphazard arrangement of couch cushions, now soiled. Only Adrienne's reception desk was still where we'd left it, too large to move.

Jason stood facing the door, hands set proudly on his hips as he presided over his handiwork. When he turned around and caught sight of us, he grinned and worked his eyebrows up and down. "Well, well. The prodigal guests return. And you, too, Adrienne."

Edison was sitting on the floor fiddling with something, legs in a 'V.' He looked up. His eyes were red slits, skin ashen. "Oh, hey, guys." He seemed genuinely excited to see us. "Where have you been? What have you been up to?"

"We saw what you did." Jason smirked.

I froze.

"What have *you* been up to?" Adrienne gestured toward the barricade.

They looked at the entrance as if they hadn't noticed what they'd done to it. Just then, the doors began to rattle violently. I covered my ears. It stopped after a moment but was followed by a heavy thwack against the glass. Then a few beats of silence, broken by a hollow thump.

"Is someone out there?" Zosiah was gripping her purse.

The doors shook and someone screamed. Another thump, like something large, a deer, maybe a big dog, was hitting its flank against the glass. My God, I thought, what if it breaks?

Jason and Edison stood beside us now. We all stared, seeing nothing. We waited for something to hit the glass again.

"It could be an animal," I said.

Jason smirked at me. I wanted to slap that look right off his face. "Humans are animals."

"It's people? There are people out there?" Zosiah murmured.

But people knocked on doors. People spoke, cried for help. Except Calle wasn't speaking. I shook my head to erase the thought and all its adjacent horrors, closing my eyes for a moment. When I opened them again, Zosiah was studying me. I glanced at Jason, then Edison. Their eyes were still on the door.

"We don't know." Edison's smile was crooked. He sounded breathless, his voice wavered. "We have no idea. It's been going on like this for hours." He laughed and ran a hand through his hair.

"Yeah, this is what we've been dealing with while you all were off stuffing your faces and napping." Jason crossed his arms over his chest. He was watching us react; he liked it when we were afraid. Perhaps it made him feel powerful, covered up his own terror.

"Hey, hey," Edison started waving his arms. "C'mon, now. We're glad you all are back and that you're okay." He smiled, looking around. "Hey, where's the other one?"

I clutched at the strap of my messenger bag and stared at my feet. Ruth, I thought. Her name was Ruth.

No one said anything for what felt like a very long time.

"She's gone," Adrienne announced matter-of-factly.

Jason's smirk turned to scowl. "What do you mean, 'gone?' Where did she 'go'?"

"We don't know." Zosiah stepped closer to Jason, one hip jutting out. "She just disappeared. She's probably still here somewhere." She tossed her hair.

"Yeah," I blurted out, "she was probably pretty upset about what you did to her girlfriend." My face went hot. Zosiah shook her head.

Jason stared at me. "So she just up and walked away? And that's it? 'Poof?'" He snapped his fingers.

Zosiah sighed as if she'd already told this story a hundred times. She tossed her hair again. "She said she was going to the bathroom. When she didn't come back, we went to check on her, but she wasn't there. We looked around, but we couldn't find her."

"The best way to find someone is to stay put," Edison interjected. His crazed grin was unnerving, and he stank of whiskey. I couldn't tell if he was still drunk or hysterical, or both.

The doors rattled again. Maybe it was the wind, I reasoned. Yes, this could all be some kind of storm, a byproduct of climate change, complete with all kinds of bizarre but perfectly natural, naturally occurring phenomena, the kind of thing we hadn't seen in a while but that the dinosaurs or woolly mammoths had learned to put up with. Of course, all those creatures were now extinct. Still, I told myself, just because it sounded like someone was desperately trying to open the door didn't mean that was the case. It didn't mean being stuck in here was better than what was out there. It didn't necessarily mean anything at all; it was just a sound. A sound that was not distinctly human in any way.

But I could not help but think about how easy it would be for an actual person, if that was indeed what was out there, to simply break the glass. Why wouldn't they? And then, would the fog rush in like water through the broken window of a sunken ship? Or would it slowly creep in like a vapor? Would we be able to breathe? How were we even breathing now? I was panting, I realized.

"Can we get out of this room?" I was grateful Zosiah said it first.

"Yes, of course," Edison beamed at her.

"We've been just fine in here," Jason grumbled. But he moved along.

The windowless office stank of booze, puke, and sweat. We stood in a little herd, looking around at the floor, scattered with papers and folders.

"It's okay, sit, sit," Edison urged us.

I was tired, so I slowly lowered myself down. Adrienne did the same, a resigned look on her face. Zosiah half sat on top of me and I lifted my shoulders back, tried to hold myself still.

"Oops," she smiled at me and giggled. Jason was watching us. She was performing for him.

Unfazed, he said, "Maybe I should go look for your friend."

"Leave her alone," Adrienne snapped. "She'll come back when she's ready."

I saw Ruth passing through that door into the final stairway up to the roof. What happened when she got up there? Maybe she didn't go. Maybe she was just sitting on the stairs, waiting for this to be over. I knew that wasn't true, though.

"Well maybe I should go scope out room 222. Maybe that's where your friend is."

"Just leave her be," thundered Adrienne.

Jason stood up and leaned over her. "You wanna come with me?"

"Absolutely . . . not." She smiled up at him as she stuck her middle finger in his face. I sucked in my breath.

Jason grinned, cocked his head. He backed away slowly, keeping his eyes on her as she glared at him in return, till he reached the door and slipped out of the room.

I closed my eyes for a moment and saw Ruth again. This time she smiled at me with such overwhelming benevolence, it hurt to behold. I wanted to write down her face, but in an instant the vision was gone.

I'd written my way through recesses, school assemblies, and standardized tests, like parallel time travel, there but not there, my hand aching as I scrawled page after page. I couldn't hold a pen now. My body was thrumming. I tried to slow my breathing.

"Hey, why the long faces?" Edison called cheerfully. "I'm sure she's okay. They'll both be okay." He sighed. "As long as we all stay in here, we'll be fine." He paused, considering this, and his smile fell, revealing his true face.

"Got any more whiskey?" Zosiah asked, her voice breathy and low.

"Uhm," Edison replied. I knew it was all gone.

"There's liquor in the kitchen. And more wine," Adrienne offered.

"Sure, sure." Edison bobbed his head. "Let's just wait till Jason gets back."

"Actually," Adrienne stood up, "Why don't we go now? We're not doing anything."

"No." Edison slapped his palm against his thigh. "Son of a bitch, I'm still in charge here. And I say you all aren't going away by yourselves again."

Adrienne surprised me when she sat back down without a word. Edison laughed nervously, running both hands through his hair.

We waited. I breathed hard, sweated, shook. Zosiah watched me. Her face said she could use a drink. It also said she was getting out of this room. *Are you in?* I glanced at Adrienne. She was studying the ceiling.

We didn't have to wait long for Jason. I heard him coming, the clunk of his shoes and the jingle of whatever he had in his pockets as he ran. He arrived panting.

"What the fuck is wrong with you people?" He glared at me.

"What's wrong with us?" Adrienne jumped up and rushed at him. She jabbed his chest with her finger. Zosiah came up behind her, though I wasn't sure if she was going to help her or hold her back. "What's wrong with you? Huh?"

Jason looked confused. "What the fuck are you talking about? First," he counted our mistakes on his thick fingers, "you lose someone. A guest, actually. Isn't it your job to take care of guests?"

"Isn't it your job to spy on them and jerk off?"

Time stopped.

A voyeur—of course. Jason's face went scarlet. His eyeballs bulged, and his brows disappeared under his hair. It was a horrible visage to behold.

"Hey!" Edison suddenly sprang to life.

"And then you gave her a key," Jason went on, still counting on his fingers. "You must've. Cuz guess what? I went to room 222, and there's no one there."

Adrienne set her hands on her hips.

"What?" I said.

"That's right. She's running around here somewhere. Ten stories, almost a hundred rooms, not to mention all the other nooks and crannies." Jason scanned the office as if Calle could be hiding there in plain sight. "Do you know how long it could take to find her? She could compromise the integrity of this entire building!"

I rolled my eyes. "Why are you so worried about the building's integrity? How does a building even have integrity? You're just anthropomorphizing."

Jason glowered at me. "Anthropo-what?"

Zosiah laughed. It was high-pitched and too loud.

"So maybe she's gone, then," Adrienne went on. "And look! No one's dead yet."

Except, maybe someone was. Adrienne had the same thought: her eye twitched.

Overhead, the lights flickered manically. Jason took a step back. He tilted his head and smirked. "Not yet."

Zosiah wasn't laughing any more. She stayed close to the wall, eyes on Jason, one hand gripping her purse strap. Adrienne stepped forward again. Jason was leading her toward the door.

"Is that a threat?"

"I'm just being realistic. You and your friends put us all at risk."

Adrienne shrugged. "So what are you going to do? What's your plan, since you're the security expert?"

Jason performed an exaggerated shrug, imitating her. "I guess you'll see."

"The plan should be to find both of them, and bring them back here." Edison said. "Jason and I will go. The rest of you stay here."

"Yeah," Jason looked down at me. "Why don't the ladies stay here?"

"No fuck—" Adrienne began, and then the lights went out.

X

In the darkness, I opened my eyes wide and a face appeared before me. Soft-lit, feminine, strangely familiar yet unknown, looking down at me with quiet concern. I squeezed my eyes shut. The face disappeared. The blackness behind my eyes was warm, red prickles of light floating mid-air. It didn't matter if my eyes were open or not, there was always another side to see.

My bag secure across my chest, I scrambled to my feet, hit something, someone. A hand snatched at my hip. There were gasps, heavy breathing, followed by shrieks, a scuffling. Something hit me in the jaw. I heard breaking glass. On my hands and knees, I crawled in the direction of the door, or what I thought was the door. Something crunched, fingers under my knee. I yelled for Adrienne, Zosiah.

"Run!" It was Adrienne's voice. Then a "huh!" sound, followed by a man's groan.

Someone grabbed my arm, pulled me up, pulled me out. Soon we were running, half stumbling, scrambling to hold onto each other. I extended my free arm straight out into the black.

"Who are you?" I panted.

"It's me."

"Adrienne! Where's Adrienne?"

Just then I heard a shuffling behind me, followed by labored breaths. "I'm coming!"

Zosiah and I paused, arms wrapped around each other's waists. "C'mon!"

The shuffling grew louder, faster. Adrienne barreled right into us, knocking us down. We climbed to our feet and lurched forward.

Behind us, Jason bellowed. "Where do you think you're going? I have all the keys! Every door has a key, you cunts, and I've got them all!"

"This way!" Adrienne hissed. We careened around a corner. I slammed into the wall but kept going. I couldn't tell how fast I was moving.

"Wait, my phone has a flashlight!" Zosiah said.

Adrienne shushed her. "Not yet! They'll see it."

We went on, pushed through a door. I could tell from the sound of it closing, plus the cool air and the feel of the floor, that we were back in the stairwell.

"More stairs?"

"Here." Adrienne's phone lit up. The light made me wince. "The elevators won't work now."

Zosiah looked around. "We gotta keep moving."

"I know, I know. Let me think." Adrienne was panting, sweating. I noticed a dark smear across her face. Blood.

"Are you okay?"

She waved the question off. In the dim light, I did my best to examine her. Her clothes were intact. I didn't see any blood besides what was on her face. I leaned in, squinting, searching for a cut or scrape.

"It's not mine, okay?" Adrienne used both hands to push me away. I retreated, wounded, but telling myself I didn't have a right to be.

Zosiah stood there waiting, feet hips' width apart. I couldn't remember the last time I'd seen her shoes. There were buttons missing off her blouse, which hung open to reveal a lacy white bra. She was gripping her purse. "C'mon, c'mon," she said quietly, shifting her weight from foot to foot.

I listened for footsteps in the hall, for the shouts or the breath of someone running full-tilt toward us.

"All right, let's go." Adrienne started down the stairs, using her phone to light the way as she led us farther into the depths of the hotel.

"Where are we going?" I whispered. "Back to the kitchen?"

"Hurry," she said.

We descended two floors, then exited the stairwell. A sharp right, then a left.

"Here we are." Adrienne pushed open a door, shone her phone-turned-flashlight around. There were rows of gleaming washing machines, a whole wall of industrial-sized dryers, two long tables set up in between, stacked with folded towels, next to piles of the not-yet-folded.

"The laundry room?" Zosiah pulled out her phone, too and waved it about. "Is there any way out from here? Is there a bathroom down here? Food, water?"

"There's a sink." Adrienne pointed at a large basin at the back of the room. "And there's a bathroom down the hall.

For now, we need to just stay in here. We can hide inside the machines. See?" She lifted herself backwards into one of the dryers, then pulled the door closed.

"We can cover ourselves with towels," I offered.

"Yeah, good idea." Adrienne popped out of the machine, grabbed an armful, and threw them in.

"We should space them out. If they're all empty except those three, it'll be obvious."

Adrienne and I began stuffing the machines.

Zosiah hung back. "We're just sitting ducks down here."

Adrienne shoved another armload of towels into a machine. "Look, they're gonna check all the guests' rooms first, okay? You heard Jason. Between the two of them, they have keys to everything. Do you want to hide in a dryer for a few hours, or do you want to get locked up in a room? Or worse? That asshole is barely a bouncer but he thinks he owns this place, and everything in it. This is his wet dream come true. Now that Calle's loose, there's no keeping him in check."

Loose. Like a zoo animal.

Zosiah thought for a moment. "Okay."

"Good, then help us."

We continued filling dryers until the tables were clear. Then we each selected a machine and climbed in, closing the doors behind us. I burrowed down. It was a tight fit, at least for me. The room was dark and silent except for my own breath in my ears. I thought to pray, but didn't know the words to any prayers. I realized Zosiah might, that maybe she was saying them in her mind right now, casting an invisible web over us. The image was comforting. I closed my eyes and tried to picture myself from above, inside this room, beneath the net of her prayer. Then I saw Ruth, peering in at me through the dryer door window, her soft-cheeked face full of earnestness and hope that hardened into resolve before my eyes. We were trapped. I felt a weight on my chest, holding me down.

I must've fallen asleep because I woke to total darkness. I flailed and slammed my hand against the dryer door. All my muscles now ached and my legs were asleep. Slowly, I pushed the door open and maneuvered one leg, then the other out of my nest of towels, till my feet were hanging over the side, dangling above the floor.

I stood up and immediately fell over with a crash. A dryer across the room popped open. Its occupant shone a light right in my face and shushed me.

"How long have we been in here?" I hissed.

The light went off. A pause.

"Couple hours," Adrienne said. I heard her climb out of the dryer. Her phone lit up again as she made her way down the aisle toward Zosiah's dryer. When she found the right one, she knocked on the door. There was no answer. Adrienne opened it and stuck her hand inside.

"Ow! She bit me."

Zosiah's head popped out of the machine. "Sorry, I didn't know it was you."

Without a word, Adrienne went to the back of the room to wash her arm in the basin.

Zosiah blinded me with her phone. "Sorry."

I scooted across the floor till I was under one of the tables all the towels had been stacked atop. Zosiah plopped down next to me. She stretched out her legs, bending forward to reach for her toes. Suddenly she jerked back and gripped her wrist.

"My bracelet," she said. "It's gone." She spun around, jumped up, and started pawing through her dryer. I wanted to help but I was held down by pain and fatigue.

"What are you guys doing?" Adrienne flashed her phone at Zosiah.

"I'm down here." I waved to her.

"My bracelet is gone," Zosiah cried. She pressed the heels of her palms against her eyes. "I know, it doesn't fucking matter." Her voice cracked.

Adrienne squatted down beside me, saying nothing. I was at a loss myself. The bracelet had caught my eye many times, but I couldn't recall when I'd last seen it.

Eventually, Zosiah went quiet and got down on the floor, too.

Adrienne turned off her phone's flashlight. "We've gotta conserve the batteries."

"Do you think they're coming down here? Did they already come through? I fell asleep," I admitted.

"No." Adrienne's shirt rustled as she shook her head. "They haven't been in here. Not yet."

Zosiah moved in closer, pressing her body against me. I could feel her breast on my arm. I held still.

"They're gonna find us, you know." She was quiet. She didn't sound afraid, only sad.

Adrienne shook her head. "Not if we stay one step ahead of them."

"When they come, I'll go with them," Zosiah said. "You two run, I'll surrender myself, or whatever. I don't mind. Really."

I maneuvered my arm around Zosiah's shoulders. She pressed her face into my collar, stuck her purse in my lap. I could feel her hot, moist mouth on my skin. She was shaking.

"You're being ridiculous," I said as she cried silently, wetting my chest.

"I just want my mother." She spoke quietly, her voice a rustle in my ear. "I just miss her."

I tried to picture my own mother, busying herself about my parents' house, cleaning things that were already clean, monologuing at my father, who muttered in reply.

It dawned on me I might not ever see her again.

"My parents are gone," Adrienne said matter-of-factly. She stuck her hands in her pockets as she raised her shoulders to her ears. "They left me with my aunt, then she threw me out."

Zosiah bawled.

I didn't know what to say. All the adults who were supposed to love Adrienne and care for her had rejected her, and yet somehow she still knew who she was. She didn't want or need my pity. I admired her.

Zosiah's sobs filled the space between us. Gently, I pulled her closer, pressed my face against her head, felt the black silk of her hair on my skin. I inhaled her scent: stale, spicy perfume, plus sweat, and a note of cheese. I recalled our excursion to the kitchen earlier, when Ruth was still with us.

Adrienne was frowning down at the floor, arms crossed. I reached out a hand to her but she acted like she didn't see it.

Suddenly, a sound in the hallway: moaning. Zosiah went rigid. We held our breath, waiting. Someone was crying; it was getting closer. Adrienne scampered off. A moment later, I heard a dryer close. I held onto Zosiah. They were right on top of us. There wasn't time for both of us to get back inside the dryers without being heard.

"Stay here," I whispered in her ear.

"No." She started to get up, but I pulled her back down to the floor.

"You don't know who it is."

I crawled over to the door. The wailing grew louder, then faded a little.

"Help," the voice moaned, drawing the word out. It was strained, raspy. I couldn't quite make out who it was, but it sounded like a man.

Slowly, I opened the door and slipped into the corridor, my back pressed against the wall. I waited, listening.

"Heeeelllp."

I moved toward the voice, praying Zosiah would stay put and give up on her plan to sacrifice herself. I knew what she was thinking: it can't be any worse. *Yes it can*, I thought.

The ceiling lit up. A ball of light flitted about, then drifted down the wall to rest at my feet. I looked up. It was Edison, holding a flashlight. I caught a glimpse of his face before he blinded me. His eyes were swollen, barely open, his hair mussed. There was an angry scratch across his cheek, in addition to the bruise on his jaw.

Edison grabbed me by my shirt collar and shoved me into the wall. "You gotta help me," he wheezed as he slammed my back and head against the plaster over and over. My vision prickled, the edges fading out. "Please. Help me." He was near weeping, his voice thick with mucous.

"I'll help you, I'll help you," I rasped. "Just stop pushing me."

He let me go, and I slid down to the floor. I lay there for a moment, curled up, breathless, in a ball.

"What happened to you?" I gasped.

Edison raised the light to my face, and I squinted, eyes tearing.

"I gotta get the hell out of here." His clothes rustled. He said something else in a language I didn't understand.

"Where are they?"

I shrugged. "They took off, left me behind."

"Bullshit."

"They did. They're going their own way."

Edison stuck two fingers in his mouth and whistled. I heard someone jogging toward us. *Shit.*

"What have we here? You found one of our friends?" Jason chuckled to himself.

Edison jerked his thumb in my direction, looked me over quickly. "Says they aren't here."

"Bullshit."

"That's what I say."

"Look," I cut in, talking fast, "they went off on their own. Frankly, I don't really blame them. I've just been a burden to them. I'm all banged up, I can barely walk. So, I don't know where they are. But I've spent a lot of time with them. They're not going anywhere. If you're worried they're going to do something stupid like go outside, you can relax. There's no way they'd do that."

"You don't know where they are? Even though you've spent all day palling around with them? They just up and dumped you, just like that?"

"Well," I cleared my throat, "they had a good scare. You know, upstairs. When the lights went out. And two is easier than three."

Jason laughed. "Yeah, ain't that the truth." *How would you know, fuckwad?* "Well," he sighed, "let's check out your story, see if you're telling the truth. You search the hall," he turned to Edison, "I'll check the laundry room. Meanwhile," he lit up my face, and I shut my eyes, "you stay here." He pointed to the carpet.

I nodded. I didn't know what else to do. They marched off on their respective missions, sweeping the floors and walls with their flashlights. I watched, paralyzed, as Jason sauntered down the hall and pulled the laundry room door open with a flourish. They had to have heard him coming. I prayed Zosiah had climbed back inside one of the dryers. I held my breath, started counting the seconds. Jason banged machines open, shoved the table around, its feet screeching in protest. *Oh God. Please God. I don't believe in you, but please, do something. Get up off your ass, that's enough for today, they've suffered enough. Time to wrap it up.*

The laundry room door flew open. Jason's flashlight appeared first, the shadow of his body behind it. I couldn't see if he had anyone with him.

"Well, that was a surprise." He knelt down close to me so I could smell his sour breath. A finger jabbed me in the ribs. I winced. "I guess you were telling the truth." He whistled, and Edison came trotting back.

"I don't see anybody," Edison said.

Jason shook his head. "I told you they wouldn't be stupid enough to come down here. You can't even lock the doors." He clapped me on the shoulder, and I jumped. "You can come with us." He pulled me to my feet. "Party of three. Well," he laughed, "maybe two-and-a-half."

XI

Jason lighted the way. I followed, and Edison brought up the rear. Officially, we were searching for Ruth and Calle. Both was the goal, though one would suffice in accomplishing the mission, apparently. There was no strategy. We marched on, turning now and then at random through what seemed like one dark, interminable hall. I thought of the minotaur, lying in wait at the center of his labyrinth, unsuspecting youths walking right into his mouth. I was thirsty, tired. My whole body ached, and it wouldn't let me forget it as we trotted through the hotel, using up the last of our strength.

I imagined Ruth had opened the door to a wall of fog. I saw her pass into it and disappear. From within, she called to Calle. She didn't sound afraid. Calle, loose somewhere, her hands feeling along the walls in the dark, searching for an exit, gasping for breath, her heart pounding. If Calle was still hell-bent on leaving the hotel, she had probably done so by now. And yet we were all alive. She probably wouldn't try to find Ruth when she got out. She would go to her son, then her husband; if she made it far enough, she'd go back to her old life, assuming it was there to go back to.

Edison sighed once, then again after a few more paces. Soon he was sighing rhythmically. I started counting the steps in between. One two three, sigh. One two three, sigh. It was the only other sound aside from the crush of feet against the carpet and the rustling of our pant legs.

"What?" Jason wheeled around, blinding me with his flashlight again as he zeroed in on Edison. "What's the problem? Why are you doing that?"

"Doing what?"

"You keep sighing! Or is it you?" Jason sneered at me.

"It's not me."

"A man can't sigh? Jesus!" Edison leaned his forehead against the wall, then stepped back and punched it, leaving a dent the size of my face. He gritted his teeth against the pain. I gaped at him.

Jason lit up the hole in the wall, then Edison's face, then the hole again. He scowled.

"Maybe you should just stay here. I'll find them myself. You're no help, anyway."

"What's that supposed to mean?"

"It means if it weren't for you and your hands-off managerial bullshit, we could've kept everybody together and I wouldn't have to bust my ass right now humping around this hotel, looking for some idiots who are going to get us all killed."

"Hey," I said, "we could all use a respite. Why don't we take a break and go by the kitchen? Refresh ourselves, then return to the mission?"

Jason scowled. "Why do you talk like that? You got a dick, anyway, or what?"

I sucked in my breath. My voice came out in a hiss. "What did you just say?" *Yeah Jason, I got a dick. I could have ten cocks in fun colors, and they'd never go soft. A dick is a dick is a dick.*

"I haven't eaten all day," Edison cut me off. He'd forgotten Calle's omelet. "Let's go." He started forward.

"Wait." Jason held up a hand. "We already searched the kitchen. There's no point in all of us trekking down there. You two bitches stay here, I'll go and bring food back."

I was shaking with rage. But I didn't want to be alone with Jason, so I said nothing. We watched the ball of light his flashlight cast dance around the hall as he walked, illuminating his foot, a hand, the hem of his coveralls, till he turned a corner and disappeared into the black. I imagined him coming upon Adrienne alone, the two of them facing off, and felt a desire to bash his face in. Suddenly, I regretted staying behind. But if I'd taken off just then, Edison would've told Jason which way I went. He might've tried to stop me as well. Soon, Jason would be after me and if I went to Adrienne and Zosiah, I'd only bring him right to them.

Edison sighed again and sat down. He turned off his flashlight. "The battery could go."

I sat down, too. It hurt every time something touched my back, but it hurt to sit unsupported as well.

We sat there on the floor, the only sound our own breathing. The building felt massive, empty, and cold. I closed my eyes, trying again to detach. *You're floating in the nothing,* I told myself. But the pain tied me down and held me there.

I decided I'd make the best of what I had, which was Edison. He might know something useful. "How long have you been working with Jason?"

He shifted his weight. "A few years, I guess. He's been here longer than I have."

I nodded, though he couldn't see me. "He's a real take-charge type."

When Edison didn't say anything, I asked him how long he'd been manager there.

"Six months."

I imagined Jason had been sullen and standoffish when Edison first took over. He wanted to get along with his staff, with the other men. He wanted friends.

"Before that, did you work in the city, or somewhere else?"

He sighed twice with pronounced annoyance. "Here," he said finally.

I decided to change course, though it took me a moment to think of what to say. All the usual questions—where do you live, etc.—seemed off limits, reminders of all the unknowns that might rev up Edison's anxiety and make him punch another wall, or me. I recalled he'd told us about his favorite soccer team, but I didn't know or care anything about soccer, so that, too, seemed like a dead end. Finally, I settled on something simple. Something that seemed unlikely to produce a violent response: I asked him his daughter's name.

He paused. "Mireya."

Meer-ay-yuh. I practiced it in my head. It sounded to me like the name of an ancient city with eroded stone steps and blue-tiled doorways. I asked him where the name came from, what it meant.

"It was my mother's name."

"In Greece?"

"No, in Ecuador."

"Oh." I blushed, hard. My god, how stupid I was. "Your English is flawless," I added, foolishly, and he grunted in response.

"Is your mother still in Ecuador?"

"She died."

I tried to picture Ecuador, but all I could conjure was a vague shape on a map, nestled between Colombia and Peru. That was it. It was an unknowable world. I didn't even know enough to ask Edison about what I didn't know. Instead, I asked him how long he'd been living in the US. I was careful to say "US," not New York.

"Twenty years."

"Wow, you must've been really young when you got here."

"Yes, I was young," Edison confirmed, with a note of exasperation. "I studied hotel management in Canada."

I wondered why he hadn't put his diploma up on the wall in his office. Was he embarrassed to manage a sex hotel? It didn't matter now.

Someone was coming. Flattened against the wall, the darkness cloaked me, or so I thought. A light hit me square in the face. Again. It was Jason.

"Still here, I see." He didn't sound surprised.

"What'd you bring?" Edison asked.

"Found some cold cuts that seemed good. Some roast chicken, too. Looks like your girlfriends went back down there. The place was in even worse shape than before." He leaned over, and I smelled beer on him.

"What friends?"

"The faucet was running, just wasting water."

I licked my lips at the mention of water. My mouth felt like I'd been eating sand.

Jason set a tray piled high with gleaming slices of meat on the floor. He stood his flashlight upright beside it, so the light reflected off the ceiling. He hadn't brought anything to drink. Perhaps Jason thought only pussies needed to remain hydrated.

"The fridge was open." Jason rolled up a slice of salami and stuffed it in his mouth. He smacked his lips. "I searched the whole floor. No sign of 'em."

Edison slipped slice after slice into his mouth, chewing noisily. I gritted my teeth.

"C'mon, eat up," Jason said. He nudged me with his elbow, and I flinched. "We gotta keep moving." I could feel his smile. He was enjoying this. The kitchen was probably just as I'd last seen it. He was making it all up to get a rise out of me.

"Do you have anyone to go home to, Jason?"

He swallowed, wiped his lips with the back of his hand. "What?"

"Edison and I were just talking about our families. Edison has a daughter, you know."

"You've got a family, then? Some . . . cats or something?"

"Do you?" I saw him lurking around the lobby, spying on Adrienne as she doodled half-heartedly at her desk.

Jason shook his head, grabbed another piece of food, and stuffed it in his mouth. He licked his fingers, reached for more. "I'm a free agent. Aren't you gonna eat anything?"

I didn't answer.

Jason shrugged. "Suit yourself."

Meanwhile, Edison was cramming my share along with his own down his gullet.

When they were finished with the meat, Jason pushed the greasy tray to the side. They both got to their feet and belched, wiped their hands on their pants, then turned and started back in the direction we'd already come. I opened my mouth, but thought better of it. If we went in circles, we'd never find anyone.

As we labored on, I concentrated on finding ways to make as much noise as possible without speaking. I took heavy steps, brushed the walls. Eventually, Jason turned and shushed me, but his "shh" was loud. I smiled to myself and went right on stomping and rustling, clearing my throat now and then.

Jason spun around. I resisted the urge to knock the flashlight out of his hand. "Shut. The. Fuck. Up."

Edison had fallen behind. He wheezed in the dark. "Let's take a break." He leaned against the wall, then slid to the floor.

Jason switched off the flashlight. "You ever been hunting?" A smile snuck into his voice. "My dad and I used to go hunting. Spent whole days crouching behind a blind, freezing our asses off. I used to think it was boring. But a good, clean shot was worth it. You don't achieve something like that by being impatient. You can't just go out there and shoot up the woods. You have to be slow, calculated. You have to think like a predator, like your life depends on making a clean kill."

"Where was this? Montana? The Alaskan wilderness?"

"All I'm saying is, it takes discipline, like any other sport."

"What kind of game did you hunt? Bigfoot?"

My head slammed into the wall. My ears rang. I pitched forward. I was falling down a well. And then I was rushing backwards through time. The walls of the hotel split open. I was back in that hallway. My eyes were open, though I couldn't see anything. I felt the wall behind me, the floor beneath me. My hand touched my forehead, wiped away sweat. I hoped it was sweat. When I was little and battling my brother's ceaseless torments, my mother used to say to me, "You have a choice." But what she really meant was, "Let him win." What she meant was, they always win.

"You should be more careful," Jason said.

Edison's breath reminded me of slow, squeaky bellows.

"Let's move out." Jason pulled me to my feet. I pushed at him and he blew me back against the wall.

"You guys. Go. Ahead," Edison rasped.

Jason shone the light on his face. "What's wrong with you?"

Edison waved the question away. "Nothing," he wheezed. "Allergy."

"Are you allergic to the food? Do you have asthma?" I crouched down next to him. "Are you in pain?" I wondered if Edison was a smoker. I hadn't seen him light up in all the time we'd been in the hotel.

Edison shook his head. His chest rose. And fell.

"We'll take you back to your office," I said.

Edison shook his head again.

"One of the rooms, then."

Another headshake.

"Well, where the fuck, then?" Jason burst in.

Edison patted the floor.

Jason started pacing. The light moved with him, spotlighting the ugly black boots he wore. Meanwhile, Edison had gone invisible, swallowed up by the pitch.

"Do you have an inhaler in your office?"

"For fuck's sake, he doesn't have asthma!" Jason kept on pacing.

I considered offering to take Edison somewhere and watch over him, but then Jason would be loose alone. Instead, I suggested I stay in the hallway with him. Jason refused with a violent shake of his head.

"Then you stay here," I shot back.

"Fuck you."

Meanwhile, Edison's breathing was growing more ragged.

"We'll come back for him." Jason sounded worn out.

I reached out to stroke the top of Edison's head but he looked up at me, one red eye squinting, and I thought better of it.

We left him there. In the dark, clutching at his flashlight, which was turned off to conserve the battery. I wanted to take it from him but I couldn't bring myself to do it. I wasn't sure I could've pried it from his hands anyway. His weary breaths followed us, echoing down the hall. Jason moved fast, fleeing that sound, and I half ran to keep up with him.

We turned a corner, then another. Finally, I couldn't hear Edison anymore. We'd either gotten too far away, or he'd gone quiet.

And now, there were two.

XII

Jason marched ahead with his flashlight held up like a torch. He wore a determined expression and leaned slightly forward as he walked, shoulders jutting out over his feet. I was two steps behind. We didn't speak. Theoretically the others could've been in any of the rooms we passed without so much as trying the knobs. It was a fucked up version of Hide and Go Seek, where the Seek part never ended. Because if we found them and the game ended, then what? It was all a ruse designed to keep his mind and body occupied with some semblance of purpose.

I slowed down. Jason kept on at the same pace. The more I lagged, the less I could see, and the slower I went in turn, until I was barely moving, my hands outstretched.

Jason growled at me to hurry up. But I couldn't.

"I need water."

"Fine."

Just like that, he opened the door to one of the rooms and went in. I was dumbfounded. We'd been walking by these rooms for so long, seemingly the same ones, it had started to feel like the doors weren't even real and now Jason had passed through one like a veritable portal into another dimension. I followed him.

In the hall, the darkness was stretched thin, broken in places by the flashlight's rays. It varied in quality, colder and deeper in pockets, till you passed through to a slightly warmer spot, the blackness thinning out. The darkness in this room was thick as pudding.

I felt for the wall, then pressed my back against it and side-stepped my way in, one arm extended in case I bumped up against a piece of furniture. My shirt snagged on the light switch. It clicked uselessly.

A spot of light landed on my foot. I stopped.

"Keep going. You're almost there."

I tried to figure out where he was in the room. I told him I couldn't see, though obviously he already knew that, but I wanted to keep him talking. Jason just laughed.

The light retracted and the room went completely black. I continued shuffling along. I was going to hit some furniture soon, I was sure of it. I had to step toward the center of the room, toward Jason.

"I just want some water. Can you shine the light on the bathroom door?"

"You afraid of the dark?"

I sighed, then struck out for the middle, holding out both arms. I made it a few steps before I hit something. It felt like a chair. I touched a cold hand. There was someone in the chair. Their skin was stiff, silky. It was Calle, she was dead. I screamed and jumped back. Jason was laughing hysterically.

"Turn on the light!" I shouted, meaning the flashlight. I couldn't see, I couldn't move. He wouldn't stop laughing.

"Turn it on!" I screamed.

"All right, all right." Jason shone the light on a chair. There was a figure sitting there, naked, wide-eyed, with reflective, chemical blond hair. Jason guffawed some more. It was a doll. Slowly, the light traveled around the room. It was full of sex dolls. Some were nude like the one in the chair, complete with pink jelly bean nipples and a landing strip of Barbie pubic hair. Others wore bras and panties, bustiers, garters and stockings, silk masks. There were even platform heels strapped to some of their tiny, arch-less feet. They were tangled together, legs wrapped like scarves around each other's necks, their mouths locked in what were probably supposed to be orgiastic 'O's of surprise. But the combined effect of their bright, marble eyes and gaping, toothless mouths was one of horror beneath the synthetic fringe of their wigs.

Jason was sitting on a twin bed in the corner, holding the light. He was still chuckling to himself.

"Where's the bathroom?"

He shone the light on a door at the far end of the room. I felt my way around, accidentally groping more artificial flesh until I found the sink. What was this room called, the Dollhouse? I found the sink when my knee bumped the cabinet below. I groaned.

I turned on the faucet and plunged my hands into the water, scrubbing at them with my nails. Then I cupped my palms and began to drink greedily. It tasted a little like sweat and metal, but it was cold and delicious all the same. I wet my whole face, washed away traces of berry pie, soaking the front of my torn shirt in the process. I didn't care. I longed for a hot shower. There had to be a tub in that room. But I couldn't bathe naked in the dark, with Jason right outside the door. I shut off the water and felt my way back into the sex doll jungle. I prayed that Jason hadn't moved things around while I was gone.

"Let's go," I said from the doorway. The flashlight was off. Jason didn't answer.

I called out, "Are you here?" Nothing.

My pulse picked up. He was hiding, in this room of all places. My breathing got faster, louder. I pawed at the bathroom door till I found the doorknob. The little lock button jutted into my palm.

I pictured Adrienne: the impassive expression behind her glasses, her dark hair piled atop her head. She was watching me right now, shaking her head.

"They're just toys," she'd say. "Get ahold of yourself." She and Zosiah were somewhere in this hotel. If Jason was going to ambush me, then there was a chance I'd be able to get past him. But what if Adrienne and Zosiah had moved on from the laundry room? Wherever they were, if they heard me coming, how would they know who it was, that it wasn't a trap, like Edison's weeping? Although now that I'd seen him punch a wall and curl up, wheezing, on the hallway floor, I wasn't so sure those tears had been fake.

Just as I was planning my move out of the room, I heard a familiar whistle in the hallway. My heart sank.

"You ready to go?" He stood in the doorway, shone the light in my eyes for the umpteenth time. I held up my hand. "C'mon."

"Oh, sorry, am I keeping you?"

He kept the light on my face. I shut my eyes against it but I could still see an ombre of electric moons.

"What? C'mon, let's go."

"Go where?"

He paused, his incredulity growing with the silence. "What do you mean, where? Stop wasting my fucking time, and let's go."

Slowly, my eyes still closed, I said, "I'm not going with you."

"What?" I heard him take a step toward me.

I jumped back into the bathroom and slammed the door. Click. It was locked. Jason pounded on it.

"Go on without me," I called.

He cursed me. He banged his fists and kicked.

"You're never going to find them," I shouted. "And you know it. Just go pick a nice, comfortable room and stay there."

Jason stopped abusing the door. I waited, listening for footsteps, heavy breathing. But there was nothing.

A thud, followed by a sigh.

"C'mon, don't do this to me." All his smirking bravado was gone. In its stead was a small, pleading voice.

"Why don't you go check on Edison?"

He kicked the door again half-heartedly. "Fuck him."

I didn't say anything more. I felt around for the toilet, made sure the lid was closed, then sat with a sigh. There had to be towels in the bathroom, a bathmat at least. I could line the tub, then curl up and go to sleep. And by the time I woke up . . . What would be different? Sooner or later, I'd still have to leave this room. Or wait for someone else to come in. My childhood home had locks like this one on the bathroom doors, little push buttons you could pop open with the straightened end of a wire coat hanger, culled from my mother's closet, after she'd been in there too long and didn't answer the initially tentative, then increasingly frantic knocks on the door. *Not again. Not again.* All Jason had to do was go get a piece of wire. I hadn't thought this through.

He hit the door a little harder this time. "Don't do this to me."

I leaned forward on the toilet seat, all my energy concentrated on listening, my eyes stretched as wide as they'd go, as if particles of sound might snag on my lashes.

He said it again. *Don't do this to me.* His voice had shrunk. I pictured him curled up outside the bathroom door, his head in his hands. He was afraid to be alone. Something hit the wood, his fist maybe. I opened my mouth, but nothing came out.

I got up and began feeling around for something I could barricade the door with, but there was nothing. I paused, listened for movement outside the room. Silence.

I piled some towels on top of the toilet as a cushion and slowly sat back down, emitting an involuntary groan as I did.

Something scratched against the door. I waited.

"Jason?" Nothing. I shifted my weight, searching for some semblance of comfort. I thought about lying on the floor.

Another scratch at the door, slow, like a single nail tracing the frame, followed by frantic pawing—a cat trapped inside a closet. I told myself it was not an animal, it was Jason.

I crossed my arms over my chest and gripped my shoulders. I missed my apartment: the window looking out onto the street and the brick face of the apartment building on the other side. I had never known what homesickness was until that moment: that longing that makes everything around you seem foreign, a replica of life. "Home" was too hot in the winter, the radiator clinking and clanking, the knob a fiery coal. You couldn't turn it down without a potholder, and even then, it did no good. The place was an inferno in summer, too. We set up fans in both the windows, which only blew in more hot air. I didn't want to go back there, I wanted to get back to the feeling of *there*.

My messenger bag was gone. Frantic, I tried to remember where I had last taken it off. The laundry room—it had to be there. Where else could it be? I was breathing too loudly. I'd made a fine trap for myself.

Jason had gone quiet. Then he sniffled. "Don't do this to me." His face was right up against the door, lips to the wood.

I held my breath. I heard a stifled sob, then silence. More sniffling, snuffling, and finally a full-on cry. He was weeping, a deluge, gulping air and hiccupping. I couldn't comprehend what was happening. I put my hand against the door.

"Jason?"

Suddenly, the lock popped. Bing! The door burst open and hit me in the head. I fell. In a second he was on top of me, holding me down, pressing my face against the floor, grinding my teeth to dust on the tile, his knee in my back. He was laughing.

"You think I can't open a stupid little lock like this?" Jason leaned in, breath hot on my face. I could taste the humid scuzz of his mouth, a near-kiss. His lips brushed my cheek. His skin was cold and wet. Maybe he really had been crying. He was in a panic, a cornered beast. He was no more in control than I was. "What are you doing in this hotel, huh? You freak." He chuckled. I was full of terror and hatred at once, a vile brew.

He used his weight to press me down harder, crushing the breath from my lungs. Then he climbed off me with a snort. I sat up fast.

"You're a pathetic piece of shit."

He laughed it off. I couldn't see his face, but I decided then the tears were real. What a burden it was, to be a man such as this. My throat was coated with acid. I felt like spitting. I had to get out of that room.

"I need to go back and check on Edison."

"Go back?" Jason was incredulous, as if we'd journeyed thousands of miles and now I was suggesting we turn around.

"We shouldn't have left him there in the first place. We shouldn't have left anyone behind."

I braced myself. I was waiting for him to say "integrity" again.

But after a minute, all he said was, "Fine. We'll go check."

Jason turned the light on me again, then yanked me up by my collar. He pushed me out the door and through the room, marching along behind me, gripping what was left of my shirt as he aimed the light over my shoulder into the paralyzed eyes of the dolls. They gleamed back at us. I shuddered as we passed heaps of their petite bodies, skeins of artificial hair streaming over cutlets of jelly flesh.

Jason closed the door behind us. He nudged me forward, back the way we'd come, shining the light on the floor between my feet. We turned into the stairwell and headed down. I half stumbled along the way. Then we passed through a winding hall. In a few minutes, we were there, at the same spot. I knew it was the place because my foot made a tinny "ding" when it hit the empty tray.

Jason waved the light around. Edison was gone, which didn't surprise me, despite the dire condition in which we'd left him. All day, people had been disappearing. Here was one more.

Jason went on wielding the flashlight haphazardly, as if there was anything to see. I checked for my messenger bag again, but it wasn't there. It had to be in the laundry room, maybe in the machine I'd burrowed inside.

Jason started pacing the length of the hallway, taking the light with him. He traveled a little farther away each time. My mother wore down our kitchen floor that way.

"He's not here," I said. Which meant he wasn't dead. At least, he wasn't dead here. I had to admit it was possible he was dead somewhere else in the hotel. "Maybe he went back to his office."

Jason ignored me and continued pacing. I thought about making a run for it, but I had to either go right past him, in which case he would probably tackle me, or go back the way we'd come, and I wasn't confident I could outrun him in the dark.

"Let's just go check his office."

Jason stopped. He aimed the light up at the ceiling, his head tilted back, mouth ajar. I imagined getting a running start, then leaping through the air to kick him in the face. I heard the satisfying crunch of his teeth.

He glared at me. "All right," he nodded. "We're gonna go check his office." He said it as if it had been his idea.

Jason led the way down the stairs, while I gripped the cold metal banister, feeling around for each step. Footfall echoed hollowly against the endless coil of cement steps, each one at the precipice of darkness, the vertiginous lip of the void. It dawned on me that Edison might actually be in his office. That he might be dead in his office, or very much alive but altered in a way that was frightening and unrecognizable. I scolded myself for going along with leaving him there, wheezing and gasping for breath. *What the fuck is wrong with you?*

"What?" Jason turned, and I nearly fell on top of him. He squinted at me, aiming the light at my chest like a bull's eye. I realized I'd been mumbling aloud.

"Nothing. I didn't say anything."

He scowled, returned to the descent.

I had to come up with a plan to get away from him, get back to the laundry room, below the lobby level where Edison's office was. Maybe Zosiah and Adrienne really were still in there. Maybe they'd stayed put so I could find them.

Or maybe they'd been glad to be rid of me and were now hiding in some spot only clever Adrienne would think of, a place I'd never find, or even realize existed.

"C'mon, hurry up." Jason had gotten a few steps ahead of me. The light wasn't doing me any good from that distance.

I did my best to close the gap, so that I could at least see a little. But I had no desire to speed our progress.

XIII

The lobby was chilly, the air cold enough to make little clouds of my breath. It was silent, very still, as though no one had been there in years. Jason flashed the light around, crisscrossing the furniture piled up in front of the doors. Someone easily could've hidden within the pyre.

"Okay," he nodded, satisfied with the lackluster light show, and motioned toward Edison's office.

The door was open. Jason shone his flashlight around in a circle, then straight through the middle. I still couldn't see anything inside. It looked like the light was reflecting back at us, as if there was a mirror filling the door frame. Jason slowly extended his hand. It passed through the glass like water. The rest of him followed. I took a deep breath and crossed the threshold after him.

The room still smelled like whiskey, old vomit, and sweat. I covered my nose and mouth, breathed wetly into my palm. Something crunched under my feet. Jason slowly illuminated each corner of the near-empty room. The floor was covered in papers and manila folders, pens, paperclips, and myriad other office-related things, in addition to some empty bottles and a discarded metal flask. No Edison.

But Jason went on scanning. He was stalling. An object at my feet lit up for a second, then disappeared.

"Wait, go back."

He dropped the light at my feet, then moved it back and forth, drawing the points of a star. I saw it again, stooped to grab it. A penlight.

"What is it?"

"It's just a pen. My pen. I dropped it in here. See?" I held it up for Jason, but he scowled and turned his back to me to continue his search. I saw my chance. I turned and ran from the room, holding up the penlight just as I reached the door.

"Hey!"

I held the button down and the light came on, weak and thin but enough to get me to the stairwell. I pushed through the door, let it slam behind me, then jumped down a flight of stairs, crouching low on impact. I paused for a second in disbelief. I'd made it. Just then, Jason threw open the door. I took off. He was right behind me, shining the light on my back. I gripped the penlight but released the button, moving by feel, my eyes closed, seeing the stairs in my mind. I urged myself on, faster, faster, let go of the fear of falling because what was the worst that could happen? I'd knock myself out? *You have nothing to lose.* I pushed on. Gripping the bannister, I jumped the stairs two at a time. Behind me, Jason stumbled. He cried out in pain. I was almost at the last flight. When I reached the top, I took a deep breath and leapt. My ankle rolled, yanking the tendons. The pain was sharp. I heard Jason's footsteps behind me and lunged for the door, then rushed headlong into the hall.

I couldn't remember if the laundry room was to the left or the right. I shone the penlight around. There was a door, straight ahead. I closed it behind me as softly as I could, fumbling for a lock on the knob. There wasn't one. I surveyed the narrow space: stacks of sheets and towels. Straight ahead, a giant, white basket on wheels, the kind housekeeping would use to collect the linens. I climbed in, burying myself in the soiled sheets, stiff with semen and God knew what else, just as the door opened. I clapped my hands over my mouth.

Jason was panting, exhaling a steady stream of curses. He stood there for a moment, presumably searching the room. Then, I heard the door move again. Everything went quiet. I waited. I was scared he'd nab me as soon as I burst out of the dirty laundry. I started to count. When I got to five minutes, then I'd creep out, exit the closet, and go find the laundry room. But five minutes came and went. Jason was out there, searching the floor. I couldn't bring myself to let him catch me again. I had a light now. A weak one, but a light all the same. It was everything I needed to navigate on my own.

After ten minutes, the closet door creaked. I held my breath. My heart was wild, blood zipping with adrenaline. Someone was rummaging around. I heard footsteps coming closer, then they stopped. Someone was standing over me. I braced myself, waited for a hand to come plunging into the basket and pull me out by the hair. I closed my eyes, crouched down low, then popped up, roaring with all my strength, like a life-sized jack-in-the-box. I heard a high-pitched scream and a crash as someone fell backwards against the shelves of towels. They toppled in a soft avalanche.

I climbed out of the basket and shone the pen light around, catching a flash of an eye and black hair. Half of Zosiah's head and body were covered by a towel. I pulled it off, and she screamed again.

"Shh! It's me!"

Zosiah squinted up at me. I was careful not to shine the penlight in her eyes.

"What? What are you doing here?"

"Looking for you. Where's Adrienne?"

Zosiah pointed to her right. "She's still in there," she whispered. "We heard someone come down." She got up, throwing the towels off. She was still barefoot but had her purse at her side. She clutched it to her chest like a life vest.

"It's Jason. He chased me down here."

"Why the fuck did you bring him back down here?"

"I didn't really have a whole lot of options." I shut off the penlight.

Zosiah sighed. "I'll bring you back. Stay close to the wall. We have to go fast."

I nodded, though she couldn't see it. I reached for her hand and she clasped mine tightly.

Zosiah pulled me toward the door, leaning in close to whisper in my ear, her breath warm. "I'll go first."

With that, she disappeared into the hall. I didn't know if I was supposed to follow her. Before I could decide, she returned.

"Okay, seems clear."

"Seems?"

I took off my sneakers, wincing at the pain in my back and ankle. Zosiah pulled me into the dark corridor and we traced the wall, turned a corner. I tried to memorize the path in case I needed to do this again on my own. I didn't realize we'd arrived till she pulled me through another doorway. The room was black. Something scraped against the linoleum.

Zosiah hissed. I heard a dryer door creak open. Adrienne jumped down, bare feet slapping the floor. A flashlight suddenly illuminated the ceiling above us, the light reflecting off the glossy white finish.

"Look who I found," Zosiah said.

Adrienne nodded at me. "Welcome back."

I looked past her to the shelves, laden with supplies: oatmeal, crackers, cookies, cans of soup, beans, sardines, and vegetables, bottles of wine, olive oil, a jug of water, a box of kosher salt, along with batteries, at least five flashlights, matches, pads of paper and a set of pens. They'd clearly been busy in the time I'd been gone.

"Is my messenger bag still here by any chance?"

Adrienne pulled the bag out from under the shelf.

"I found it in your dryer."

"Thank you." I cleared my throat. I didn't know what to say after that. I rubbed at my cowlick.

Zosiah told Adrienne Jason had followed me down. She looked at me and frowned, then shrugged. "So what? We have everything we need."

"Except a bathroom."

"We have buckets. And we have water."

Zosiah shook her head. She pushed past me, purse swinging, and collected a few flashlights off the shelf. Then she set them about the room. They stood straight up, beaming warmly at the ceiling. The effect was kind of romantic.

I could make out most of the room now. A flimsy chair from Edison's office was propped up against the door. I pointed it out to Adrienne.

"If someone's pushing from the other side, it won't hold."

"I know. But it'll make noise."

"Why don't you block it with one of the washing machines?"

Adrienne shook her head. "Too hard to keep moving back and forth. Once we do that, we have to stay in here."

That didn't sound like the worst option to me, but I didn't say so. Instead, I asked Adrienne if she'd seen Edison.

"Edison?" She shot me a quizzical look. "Wasn't he with you?"

"He was."

She didn't ask what happened, so I didn't tell her.

"Jason's going to come in here. Sooner rather than later, most likely."

Adrienne set her hands on her hips. "Yeah. But if it's just him now, that's three against one. And we have a tactical advantage."

"Tactical advantage?"

She pointed at the chair sitting in front of the door. She gestured toward the flashlights, the rows of dryers, then the shelves full of supplies. "We'll hear him coming. We have all the flashlights, all the batteries. Jason isn't in a position to tell us what to do anymore." She smiled her tight, closed-lipped smile.

What was he in a position to do? *Unhinge himself. Sit on me, beat my head against the floor. Drag us all out by the hair.*

The faucet opened with a rush. Zosiah was sitting on the edge of the big-basined sink, scooping water into her mouth. I was thirsty again, watching her.

Adrienne was right. And she could certainly handle herself. But there was something about the way she was talking now, the jut of her hip, her feet set apart, that both impressed me and made me uneasy. I thought about Jason crying outside the bathroom in the sex doll room, or at least how I thought he had. Then he opened the door and hurt me. Adrienne had known him the longest and clearly thought he was a threat, but I wondered if the contempt she felt for him was clouding her judgment slightly. Maybe I knew something about Jason's shame and propensity for violence that so far he'd hidden from her: that he was petrified of being alone, and now that he was, he'd do anything to bring us back and hold onto us.

Adrienne clapped me on the shoulder. Could she hear my thoughts, or was I mumbling to myself again? "Don't worry."

But I was worried, I was definitely worried.

XIV

I sat at the back of the room near the supply shelves and scribbled a few phrases in my notebook before I put it back in my messenger bag. Next to me, Zosiah was working on a makeshift "stove": a cake pan lined with tinfoil, filled with crumpled newspaper. A cooling rack went over the top, a pot of water above that. The paper burned out too quickly for the water to get past lukewarm though.

I surveyed the room. The chair from Edison's office had wooden legs. I asked Zosiah for a knife. She hesitated, looking around. She was clutching her purse again.

"Adrienne has a kitchen knife she stashed somewhere."

I pushed myself up, put my shoes on. Without a word, I took the chair and brought my foot down right at the joint. The leg broke off, splintering. Then the chair clattered to the floor.

"Shh!" Adrienne popped her head out of one of the dryers.

"Where's that knife you stole?"

"I didn't steal it." Adrienne pointed at the box of salt.

I pulled it out and handed it to Zosiah. "Don't cut yourself," I said, channeling my mother. She never cut herself, as far as I knew. That was not her way. She took day-long baths during what my father called her "low points" but she never touched the razors. Or maybe my father removed them.

Zosiah gestured at my messenger bag with the knife. "You writing in your notebook?"

I looked down. "Writing? No. I mean, a few lines. I didn't know where it was for a while, but yes, I am. I will." I got out my notebook again and stared at the cover. Something clicked. "It's a hotel," I was talking to myself. "A hotel to cry in."

Sponge-painted in tears, crystallized salt on the walls. Of course, the rooms would have to be soundproof, too. And lush with luxury, everything top of the line from the sheets to the carpet, the pillows soft as puppies, boxes of silk tissues on the nightstand, a state-of-the-art sound system in every room playing pensive, melancholy instrumentals. The guests could wallow in their own sadness in total anonymity, without the interference of hunger or ringing telephones or housekeeping knocking at the door. A futuristic kind of dumbwaiter would deliver anything they wanted to eat directly to the room. There would have to be multiple check-in desks with assigned check-in and check-out times so that guests would never meet each other. Housekeeping would be entirely invisible, traveling through a network of tunnels and back stairways.

Zosiah chuckled. She seemed unimpressed. Sawing at the chair leg was creating more dust and splinters. Walking around barefoot in here was going to be a problem now.

"You should write about this. About me," she said.

"About you?" No one had ever asked to be one of my characters before.

"Nah, make me someone else." Zosiah sighed, wiping at her forehead with the back of her hand, still gripping the knife, the blade an inch from her skin.

"You're going to dull it like that."

She set it down. "I know. Well, it was your idea."

"A lot of my ideas don't pan out." I paused. "I don't know if I could do you justice."

She shrugged. But she didn't look at me. I worried I'd somehow hurt her. "My standards probably aren't as high as yours," she said quietly.

"I'd be honored to try."

Zosiah smiled, looked sideways at me.

I glanced at the wounded chair, lying a few feet from the door. We'd broken it for no reason.

I cleared my throat. "When I was a kid, my mother hid piles and piles of books under her bed."

Zosiah smirked. "Erotica? Romance novels?"

"One of them was called *How to Deal with a Difficult Child*."

"Oh."

"They were all like that. *Raising a Hard-to-Raise Child. The ABCs of Bringing Up a Challenging Child. A Mother's Guide to Setting Limits*, that sort of thing."

"Were you a bratty-brat, then?"

I shook my head. "No, not at all." I remembered peering under the dust ruffle at the stacks and stacks of books, their spines pristine, unbroken. The covers were glossy, the paper a bright, virginal white. She never read most of them, but she kept buying them. Over the years, more and more accumulated, till they were practically holding up the bed.

"In high school, I found a beat up copy of the DSM under there, with a dog-eared page on gender dysphoria. 'Disorder' and 'disassociation' were underlined. She'd done her homework, she consulted experts."

There were no books on gender identity, no trans or nonbinary authors in her stacks, only doctors with black and white headshots of them in their lab coats. Still, it was her way of trying: pathologizing with love. The only language she knew was "health." Most of her life, doctors had been instructing her on how to be a woman.

"At first, I thought she got them because I quit every activity she signed me up for, because I was bad at math and didn't have any friends, because I was too weird. Children sniff out difference like dogs. I didn't understand what it was about me that made me weird, though. Or difficult. I did everything I was told to. Then I found the books and I knew it was me." I paused. "My brother told his friends I thought I was a boy. They called me a dyke, and a fag, for good measure."

I told her how they'd chanted at me on the school bus in the morning and when I got off, they were right behind me.

"It's a girl, right?" "The butt looks like a girl." They looked to my brother to confirm.

"Yeah, it's my sister."

The body was a liability: soft, porous, easily broken and controlled. Shame scalded as much as hot lunch dumped in your lap.

Zosiah sucked in her breath. "Your brother? What did your mother do?"

I shook my head. I recalled her exact words. I made my voice shrill, a parody: " 'Gabe wouldn't do a thing like that.' "

"Kids tease!" my father chimed in. "Growing up, I knew a boy named Ashley. Boy, did he catch hell."

I described my mother to her, pacing the length of the kitchen. The floor was worn down in a strip from one end of the room to the other, past the sink, right up to the fridge. Her hands twitched.

Let them win. "You're right, you're both right." I forced a smile. My brother was upstairs in his room, playing video games. I went to my room and locked the door.

"Something's wrong," she told the kindly pediatrician in his white coat with liver-spotted, hairy-knuckled hands and nose hair. I was fifteen, and I'd only ever had one period. The doctor nodded at every word. He had much experience with nervous mothers.

I sat on the table in a thin gown, all but naked, hunched over, saying nothing.

"Well, let's see here," the doctor said. "Lie back." I uncurled myself slightly. He padded and probed the body as I looked at the ceiling. To possess a body is to endure, I told myself. He told us I was underweight.

"Go home and drink some milkshakes," the doctor said and smiled, his teeth oversized and yellowed as linoleum, like I was a frappe-drinking teen about to head off to the soda fountain at the town pharmacy before the weekly sock hop. Except in our quaint, white town with no synagogue but a plethora of churches, guns stashed at the back of many a closet, the pharmacy did have a lunch counter that served grilled cheese and BLTs.

At dinner, my mother served me extra meat instead of Gabe, who ate with his head down anyway so he never noticed. She ordered me to eat ice cream for dessert, demanded I take wax-covered cheese snacks and bags of mixed nuts to school. I told my mother the period came back, deposited unused pads in the trash for four days a month to convince her. She wouldn't go so far as to unroll them and check for blood, I didn't think. Not because it would disgust her, but because there was a limit to how much she wanted to know. Knowing would have meant more doctors, more tests and interviews, perhaps a therapist, a psychiatrist, maybe a few of each, and then all the bills and questions, the family sessions where her parenting would be questioned. I told Zosiah she had suffered from that level of intervention her whole life and that was where she drew the blessed line for me.

Zosiah sighed. "Jesus." Her voice was small, thoughtful.

I was thinking aloud, if only there had been volumes of advice for me, the child, on how to grow up with a mother who suffered depressive bouts where she let the garden rot and the house fill with grime and the laundry go sour, mold adding fur toes to our socks. My father, a grown-up, didn't know what to do. He brought home takeout and stayed in his study, playing with his toys. It was the only clean room in the house. Gabe went to a friend's, a kid who had a single mom who was always working and didn't know what her son was up to. As for myself, I couldn't even remember what I did, if I stayed in my room or watched TV all night or what. Probably I wrote stories about monsters and orphans locked in towers. I only remembered knowing my mother was behind that door in her bedroom, in the bath, and that she wasn't coming out, and I remembered worrying, every time, that she would never come out, that she'd never go back to caring if I was alive or dead. But she always did come back, eventually. One day, she'd be in the kitchen again, cleaning up and cooking as if nothing had happened, and when she saw me, each time, the first thing she'd do was scold me for my fingernails, or wearing the wrong shoes, or for not having brushed my hair, as if she wanted me to know she was vigilant, even when she wasn't, warning me against being different.

Every time she came back, there was a little less of her. She'd laugh a little less often, stare into space. When I hugged her, she'd hug me back, but it wouldn't feel like it. It cost her something to cross over in her mind from wherever she went, back to the minutiae of the physical world.

One day I came home from school, and the garage was closed. The door was always open. I didn't like to stand under it, afraid it would fall and crush me. I wasn't strong enough to lift it. Gabe was, but he was hanging out with his friends. I heard a car running inside but I couldn't see in; there was a fog in there, it had filled the garage. It was a clear day, cold, but sunny. The sun was in my eyes. I didn't know what was happening. I screamed and clawed at the door. I grabbed the handle, and with all the strength I could muster, I hefted it open.

I looked up at Zosiah. She was crying, messily. I realized what I'd said. "Tell me more about your mother. She sounds like good material."

Zosiah shook her head. "You saved her." Her voice snagged on a sob.

I choked on the exhaust that came pouring out when I opened the garage door. She was in there. A neighbor came running over. I was still screaming, they had to slap me to get me to stop. She didn't *want* to be saved.

"I stopped her. I didn't save her." My voice was hoarse.

Zosiah sniffed. "My mother isn't really Jewish."

"So, what is she, then?" I tried to keep my voice small.

"Nothing." *So you're nothing?* "She isn't anything. She . . . " Zosiah trailed off. Silently, she sobbed. I leaned in close and smelled her hair. She tucked in next to me, set her head on my shoulder. Her hair tickled my neck. I put my arm around her and held her. I wondered who her mother was, or if "Mother" was code for someone else.

"What was your birth name?"

"I don't know," she whispered. "They called me Lily at the American adoption agency. Like a rescue cat or something."

"How did you get there?"

She shook her head. I wasn't sure if she didn't know, or couldn't speak.

"I was named after my grandmother, my mother's dead mother." Not just the 'E' but the whole shebang. "Esther." It was still on my ID yet it had been so long since I'd said it aloud. It sounded like mothballs and needlepoint. "I don't usually tell people that." I didn't tell anyone.

"It's so . . . Jewish." Zosiah tittered.

I laughed and it hurt. "They made Jaime my middle name for some reason. It seems like a correction, like my real name was there all along, they just didn't see it."

Zosiah chuckled. She wiped at her face. "I'm sorry I lied to you."

"It's okay," I said and meant it. The truth seemed unimportant in that moment. And yet, I suddenly and inexplicably felt with absolute certainty that Zosiah's mother—whoever that was to her—was already dead and had been for a very long time. I pulled her in closer and she leaned into me.

"A family came to Korea and adopted me. And then, I don't know. Something happened. They didn't want me anymore. All I know is I was two when my parents got me."

"And they weren't Jewish?"

She covered her eyes. "No," she shook her head. "I'm sorry."

"You were pretty convincing, I have to say. But I'm no expert."

"Our neighbors were Jews. I grew up watching them, this big, noisy family. They were American, they only spoke English, but they had their own thing in their religion. I never felt Korean. My parents tried to make me learn the language but for what? They couldn't speak it. Who was I going to talk to?" she grumbled. "I didn't know anything about my birth place. So Korea was just this thing that made me stick out, marked me as an orphan, poor little Asian girl." Zosiah rolled her eyes. "I hung out with the Jewish kids, I got invited over for Shabbat dinners and Seders. It felt comfortable, it felt like . . ." She smiled. "Like New York. Like, not America, but New York. You know?"

"I know." I thought about the shirtless boys in the park, playing rugby, the faint lines under their pecs, the surgeon's signature.

Zosiah sighed, nestled in close. Her nails lightly grazed my thigh. My pulse quickened. She pressed her face to my neck and I could feel her lips on my skin. I sucked in my breath as she took my hand in hers.

"You're cold," she murmured but my face was burning. Gently, she kissed me. Her lips were silk. Then she kissed me again, a little more insistently, and when I felt her tongue between my lips, I sucked in my breath. She pressed my hand to her heart.

We fell asleep on the floor, Zosiah's head on my chest, her leg wrapped around mine.

*

A knock at the door startled us awake. Actually, not one knock but several, loud and sustained enough to wake me up from a dark well of a dream that was sucking my mind deeper and deeper into the recesses of its unreality, so that I came to with a gasp, relieved to be back in this world, only to realize this world was at my door, demanding to be let it.

Adrienne was already back inside her dryer, a gerbil in a cage. "Hide!" she hissed.

Zosiah groaned and rubbed her neck. Slowly, she sat up.
"Shut it!"

It was too late for hiding or panic. I got up.

"What are you doing?" When I didn't stop, Adrienne called me a "dumb fuck" and shut her dryer.

I opened the door. Standing before me, hands folded at his belly like a Christmas caroler, was Edison.

He smiled sheepishly. "May I come in?" His voice was raspy, faint.

I looked around. Zosiah was still sitting on the floor. I could just make her out in the dim light. Adrienne had not re-emerged from the dryer yet.

"Okay." I didn't know what else to do. The truth was, he could come in any time he wanted. We all knew it. But he'd been polite and knocked, like we were all in on a kind of make-believe. I decided to roll with it.

"Do you want something to drink?"

Edison stepped inside, squinted, looking around. "Oh, do you have water?"

I pointed in the direction of the basin at the back of the room. He thanked me, walked over to the sink, and began slowly washing his face. Then he decorously cupped the water in both hands and slurped it up. When he'd refreshed himself, he turned back to me. I stood a few feet away, Zosiah right behind me, peeping over my shoulder.

What do you say to a dead man? You could ask him how he died, how he came back, how all that went. You could ask after his dangerous asshole employee/companion to see if he knew where he was, even though they could still have been in cahoots, this whole civil entrance just a ruse, a distraction from the coming ambush. Or you could stand there staring, saying nothing, waiting for something to happen.

Edison took another look around the room, marveling at the level of organization on display. He was making me nervous. I imagined he was taking inventory of everything to report to Jason.

"Where's Adrienne?" His voice rasped like sheets of rice paper rubbing together.

Zosiah and I exchanged glances. I waited to see if Adrienne would pop out of her dryer or not. I knew she was listening. When she didn't emerge, Zosiah said, "Where's Jason?"

Edison smiled, shrugged with an air of innocence that was hard not to find convincing. He still looked tired, but the circles under his eyes had faded somewhat, and his skin was a more natural color now. Even the bruise on his jaw seemed more subdued, or maybe it was just the dim light, masking his pallor.

"I really don't know," he said.

Without a word, Zosiah picked up her purse and slipped toward the door. I winced at her bare feet, thinking of all the splinters. She peered around the corner, looked both ways, stepped into the hall, and was gone.

Edison and I regarded each other, smiled awkwardly. How had he known we were down here? I suddenly wondered. Had Jason told him? My skepticism returned, along with its invigorating jitters and stomach acid. I wanted to trap Edison in a lie, force him to reveal something without him even knowing it, but I didn't know what to ask. I wasn't good at that kind of thing.

Zosiah returned. "I didn't see anyone," she said, looking at me, ignoring Edison. She glanced at Adrienne's dryer, and I hoped Edison hadn't noticed. I didn't want us to give her away.

"I really don't know where he is," Edison went on.

"Then why are you here?" Zosiah crossed her arms.

He sighed. "I was asleep. I don't know for how long. When I woke up, I was on this floor."

We stared at him. If the story was true, it meant Jason had deposited Edison here. If it wasn't true, then it was a poor, stupid lie that made no sense. Or maybe that was exactly how it was supposed to appear. I sighed.

"Can you give us a minute, please?" Zosiah gestured toward the door.

"Oh, sure." Edison hesitated. "It's just . . . Look, I just want to say that I know things got out of hand today, but I'm really not a bad guy. I'm doing my best here, like everyone else." Wheezing, he paused, perhaps realizing his mistake. Not all of us were doing our best, obviously. Some of us were definitely doing our worst, or close to it. "I'm really not teaming up with Jason, if that's what you think. I got stuck with him, same as you." He nodded at me, to my chagrin. Zosiah looked at me.

"Okay, we'll talk to you in a minute." She held the door open for him.

"Oh, okay." He backed out of the room. If he'd had a hat, he would've held it with both hands, right over his crotch.

Zosiah closed the door, then made her way to the very back of the room, motioning for me to follow. Adrienne emerged soundlessly from her dryer and appeared at my side. I jumped.

We huddled up. Zosiah went first, whispering, "So, what do you think?" She looked at me.

Adrienne shrugged. "He's probably lying, even if he doesn't know he is." The way she saw it, the issue wasn't whether or not Edison was telling the truth, it was how we could keep control of the situation. "If we send him away," she pointed out, "then he's free to go back to Jason, and then the next time he shows up, it's the two of them."

"Like that old saying, keep your friends close, keep your enemies in a laundry room," I said. Zosiah elbowed me gently.

"I don't like this." She shook her head. "Let's keep him out, block the door."

"Oh, now you want to barricade the door?" Adrienne rolled her eyes. "What about going to the bathroom?"

I cleared my throat, then pointed out that Edison probably no longer cared about rounding people up and keeping them away from windows and doors. He was sick, I insisted. I'd seen him, on the floor, barely able to breathe. Being comfortable was likely all that concerned him.

They were quiet for a moment.

"You're probably right," Adrienne said at last. "I've worked with him for a while. He's not a bad guy."

We paused, considering this phrase again. What did it mean to be "not a bad guy" when you tied someone up against her will, left her in Jason's charge? But Zosiah had helped, I reminded myself. I glanced at her. Yet, somehow I trusted her all the same.

They sent me to bring Edison back in. I took a flashlight with me, danced the light around the hall, searching for him, but he wasn't there. I moved farther into the corridor, shining the light up and down the length of the walls in parallel stripes. I was about to call his name when I found him, sitting on the floor, his hand held up to shield his eyes from the light.

"Oh, there you are." I aimed the flashlight at his feet. "Sorry about that. They sent me to bring you back."

Edison smiled up at me, though he was wheezing, his chest expanding slowly.

"Okay," his voice was far away. He attempted to stand but slipped back to the floor. I set the flashlight down and tried to lift him up, like a child, my hands under his arms, but he was too heavy. I called for backup. Zosiah appeared in the doorway.

"What is it, what happened?" She shone her flashlight around frantically.

"Help me get him up."

Together, we managed to lift Edison to his feet. With one of his arms around each of our necks, we shuffled sideways through the door. I was sorry we'd broken the chair. Adrienne was still out of her dryer, having apparently decided to show herself. She made Edison a cushion out of towels. Slowly, we set him down, losing our grip a little as we neared the floor. He half dropped onto the towels.

"Ooey," he rasped, though he was still smiling. His breath sounded jagged, like some kind of weak, leaky mechanism, rusted and old, sharp points sticking out in places they didn't belong. He couldn't hold himself up. Adrienne made him a pillow next and fitted it under his head.

"There you are." He carefully enunciated each word. "Here I am," he rasped.

Zosiah offered Edison more water, or something to eat. He shook his head. Meanwhile, Adrienne assembled a mattress for him, folding the towels in thin layers that she fit under him one by one. Edison laid his hands atop his belly.

We stood over him, unsure what to do with ourselves now. It seemed we should've been doing something more. But what?

"The first aid kit," Adrienne offered, her eyes brightening behind her hipster glasses.

Edison shook his head. "No . . . good."

Adrienne didn't reply. The only first aid kits I'd ever seen had contained nothing but gauze, Tylenol, and Band Aids. What did he need? If he didn't have asthma or emphysema, then what was wrong with him? The question made my throat seize. But we'd been in the hotel all this time and everyone else was fine, I reasoned. Except Calle. For the first time, there was a gleam of terror in Adrienne's eyes.

Edison's breathing was slowing down bit by bit. Zosiah gripped my hand, her nails digging into my skin as his eyes fluttered closed.

Suddenly, his eyes flipped open. "I hope the lesbians are okay." He coughed and his whole body shook. Then his eyes shut again. The strangled wheezing resumed.

XV

We watched while Edison slept. He strained with the effort of each breath, the tendons standing out in his neck.

I had never before heard what is called the death rattle, though I'd read about it in novels. All the people I'd known who had died—just a handful of elderly relatives—had done so in facilities designed for that purpose, with nurses around who knew all there was to know about dying. But now I was witnessing it and it was unsettling and loud. Edison's breathing was like thick pieces of cardboard being wrenched apart. The sound was everywhere in that room. If you turned around, closed your eyes, it was still in your ear.

Adrienne tended to him patiently. She padded his body with more towels, moistened his lips now and then with a wet washcloth, wiped the sweat off his face. At one point, I saw her lift up his eyelids and shine a flashlight into his pupils. I couldn't tell how he responded or what it meant, and I didn't ask. We weren't speaking: not about what was happening in front of us, not about anything. What was there to say? That we might be next? There was no one to tell us if this was so. We'd find out in due time.

The room felt close and hot, the walls molten, the paint bubbling. I was sweating. I kept an eye on Zosiah, who had staked out a spot on top of one of the washers near the door, her back to the interior of the room. She wasn't moving. From behind, it seemed she was just staring at the wall.

I went up to her, stood close. She reached for my hand. Her eyes were swollen from crying, with dark half-moons beneath as though she hadn't slept for days. Outside in the hall, something creaked. We both stiffened. It could've been the building settling.

"He's coming back, you know," I whispered, my left cheek pressed to her right, each facing the opposite direction.

"I know."

On the floor lay Edison, laboring, limbs straight as an arrow. He still had his square-toed dress shoes on.

I heard something behind me and turned to see Adrienne standing there with her hands stuck in her back pockets, elbows jutting out.

"I think we should go get him. Just go find him now before he wanders in here," I said.

Adrienne crossed her arms.

"And then what?" Zosiah said. Her tone was skeptical, but she looked eager. She wanted to get out of that room just as badly as I did. We locked eyes. We knew we'd die in there, even if we didn't actually die. I nodded at her.

"Tie him up. Lock him in somewhere. Something like that." I imagined Jason in a metal cage too small for him to move, peeping through the bars. I felt light-headed, punchy. My clothes were sticking to me. It hurt to move at all, even to talk. I couldn't breathe. I tried not to think about breathing.

Adrienne shrugged. "If you wanna go, go ahead."

Zosiah jumped off the washer. "I'm in. I'll go."

"That's a good idea." Adrienne nodded in approval. Did she think I needed assistance, protection? I wiped at my face with my remaining shirtsleeve. She was probably right, though.

We took flashlights off the shelves and fitted them with new batteries. Zosiah secured her purse to her shoulder. I left my messenger bag on the shelf and my shoes on the floor beneath. That was it for supplies. At the threshold, I turned, peered back into the dim cavern of the laundry room. Adrienne sat on the floor next to Edison. She was looking down at him. What if Jason came in and found her alone? I wondered if Zosiah should stay. But I knew there was no way she would.

"If you find him first . . ." I trailed off. I didn't know how to finish that sentence.

Adrienne waved me toward the hall. "I'll be fine." She seemed to really believe it and that encouraged me, made me feel slightly better about leaving her alone with a severely ill man. At the same time, it made me feel a little worse.

"Be careful."

She didn't answer.

Zosiah and I turned right and began walking down the hall, moving slowly, lighting our way with her flashlight alone. For the moment, we didn't really need two. I recalled combing the halls with Edison and Jason, how they'd doubled back at random, passing door after door without even glancing inside.

"We need a plan."

Zosiah stopped. She pulled me against the wall, then down onto the carpet, her arm in mine.

"Okay, what?"

I suggested we comb the floor we were currently on, do a quick sweep of each room we passed. Then we'd go on to the next floor and the next, till we reached the top. If we still hadn't found him by then, we could move back down, floor by floor, and do a second sweep.

Zosiah didn't say anything. In that silence, I realized how long the search would take and why Edison and Jason had skipped the rooms and stuck with the halls. I also realized I really did want to find him. Or maybe it was just that I didn't want him to find us first. Still, if we wandered around for long enough, perhaps he'd pick up our scent and we could lure him away from Adrienne, which was what mattered most.

"C'mon," I said, "the hotel isn't that big."

"It's not like searching a house."

Zosiah presented an alternate plan. If we were confident Jason was going to make his way down here at some point, then why not just wait for him and cut him off? She suggested we guard the door to the stairwell along with any other points of entry, then patrol the hall. We could split up, each take one side.

"But what if he doesn't? What if he's holed up somewhere?" There were other what if's I didn't say. What if he stumbled upon one of us alone, for instance.

Zosiah's eyes lit up. "The kitchen! Jason will have to go to the kitchen sooner or later. We could just wait him out there."

And meanwhile get some food too, I thought. Maybe use it to bargain with him. I opened my mouth to voice my thought, then froze. I heard something, a scratching, scuffling sound at the end of the hall. Zosiah shut off the flashlight. We stood up, our bodies tensed, listening. Slowly, we felt our way along the wall, just as we had when Zosiah liberated me from the linen closet. When we reached the end, we turned on our flashlights, almost at once, and lit up the corridor, strobing the floor and the ceiling in wild arcs. I saw a sliver of white in the black, a flash of a dark, flat eye. Then it was gone. I shone the light again and again at the same spot but there was nothing, no one there, till I finally began to doubt what I'd seen. I turned to Zosiah. Had she seen it too? But she was still waving her flashlight around frantically. I told her to stop.

She paused and shone the light right in my eyes. I winced, held up my hand. Zosiah lowered the beam.

"What?"

"Did you see that?"

She stared. "See what?"

Then she froze. She heard it, we both did. The hush of the stairwell door closing. The door was behind me, back the way we'd come.

Without a word, we ran, flashlights aimed at the floor. It looked like the carpet was undulating under our feet.

Zosiah got to the door first. She threw it open and plunged into the dark. She fell, striking her knee on one of the steps, but quickly scrambled back up. I rushed after her, shining the light over her head, farther up the stairwell. Nothing. I tried to keep it steady as I climbed, but the flashlight swung around in front of me, rendering my vision spotty. I felt dizzy and I was breathing hard. Ahead, Zosiah's feet slapped against each metal step as she ran. She was calling to him. My heart and lungs were on fire. I paused, turned back, and shone the light down the stairwell to see how many flights I'd run. Only four.

"C'mon!" Zosiah cried. She was getting farther ahead of me.

As I looked up, I saw another flash out of the corner of my eye. A hand: pale, fingers curled, touching the bannister. I shone the light on the spot. Nothing. I started to panic. My adrenaline surged. I scrambled up the stairs after Zosiah, simultaneously chasing and running away from perhaps the very same someone. Now Zosiah was panting, too. She struggled to speak, the words coming out in strangled half-breaths. "Hurry. Hurry."

Above us, a door closed.

"There!" Zosiah cried. She skipped a step, rushed ahead toward the landing. "This one, this one!" She bent over, one hand on her knee, the other pointing at the sixth-floor entrance.

I took a deep breath, managed to expel two words in a wheeze. "This one?"

She nodded. Together, we pushed the door open and burst into the hall, waving the flashlights like loaded weapons.

"Jason!" Zosiah cried.

I didn't see anything. We bumped against each other, then sank into an exhausted heap on the floor. I shone my flashlight over the ceiling, let the light slide down the wall to the carpet. It was quiet up there, the doorways all so sleek, our breathing coarse and impossibly loud.

"Fuck."

"Now what?"

But we knew now what. We climbed to our feet. I tried the handle on the door closest to me. The room was locked. Were they locked only on this floor, or had someone gone and locked them all?

As we made our way through the hall, flashlights sweeping, Zosiah tested the doors on the left while I tried the ones on the right. I listened intently for a footstep, or a cough. I was surprised when a crystal doorknob turned in my hand and I found myself suddenly in a compartment on a luxury train from another century. I shone my flashlight over the dark wood paneling and heavy velvet drapes, like an officer searching a continental express, the artificial window looking out onto a nighttime scene of snow-capped mountains that reminded me of something I'd read in Nabokov's memoir about his mother, wrapped in furs, nestled in her sleigh laden with gifts, traveling through the Russian snows to meet her favorite boy.

The compartment seat was the bed, a dustbin tucked discreetly in the corner. The bathroom door was barely distinguishable from the wall, except for a small, brass handle. There were no chains hanging from the ceiling, no restraints attached to the bed, no giant wooden X. And yet it was somehow even creepier than the candy-colored-dildo-themed room I stumbled upon next, with glossy jelly toys mounted on the walls, bobbing their heads in greeting alongside a rainbow of dick pics in cartoon frames, unsettling for the absence of humans the set was designed to entertain.

Together, we reached the last room. The door wouldn't budge. We pressed our ears to the wood. Nothing. I knocked twice. Zosiah jumped at the sound. Still nothing.

We headed back to the stairwell, down to the next floor to resume our sweep. Now and then, Zosiah hissed "Jason!" into the dark and I winced as the sound echoed off the walls.

On the next floor, we tried two doors before the third opened. Zosiah nodded at me to go in while she stayed behind, her back to the wall, flashlight at the ready.

A button eye caught a chink of light. It belonged to a plush rocking horse with a mane of yarn. The horse wore a leather saddle with a big, veiny, bubblegum pink dildo strapped to the center. I shone the flashlight around the perimeter of the room. There were whips and crops mounted on the walls, along with framed photos of smiling women astride horses, or standing beside their chestnut steeds, gripping the reins. The photos looked old, faded, the haircuts out of date. They seemed like real pictures taken by people with pure intentions.

I stepped on something crinkly. I looked down and found an empty candy bar wrapper. Sweeping the floor, I found more wrappers, an empty bottle of water, some used napkins, and other refuse.

"Find anything?" Zosiah hissed at me from the doorway.

"C'mere."

Amongst the trash was a brown leather wallet. It must've fallen out of his pocket. Or maybe he had left it there for us to find. I lit it up for Zosiah and she snatched it off the floor. She looked like a kid on a treasure hunt.

I expected the wallet to be full of weird odds and ends, maybe some creepy school photos or telltale receipts, but there was nothing, just a few bills, bank and credit cards. The license was gone, but the name on the cards was Jason's. Zosiah tucked it into her purse.

"So, we know he was here."

"That's not very much," I said.

Zosiah shone her flashlight around the room and scowled at each horse.

XVI

We moved silently through the dark toward the stairs. Then, I heard a voice. I spun around and my flashlight moved with me, a comet's arc. I caught something. On the floor sat a pair of eyeglasses, intact, half unfolded. I stared down at them, uncomprehending. They were too thick to be Adrienne's. Someone laughed. *I'm watching you*, said a voice in my ear.

I turned around. There was no one there.

"Zosiah?"

"Yeah?" she was right beside me. We were alone.

Suddenly, I was down, pressed against the floor. My vision flashed white for a moment. I was thrashing, flailing. My head was yanked back, then hit the floor. I heard the crunch of my nose breaking as blood gushed into my mouth. I coughed and tasted the rough fibers of the carpet. They prickled my tongue.

"You're in it now." The voice growled. It was rich, sardonic, everywhere and nowhere.

From somewhere above us came a sound, the rush of a wave, looming. A chorus, laughing. It got louder. It wasn't laughter at all but cries, wails, swept up in a roar. Pounding, it towered, crescendoed, and crested over me.

*

I was clinging to the ceiling. There was a hot voice in my ear. Someone was on my back. A fine mist of spit. Sharp knees in the back, curses. The carpet beneath me was wet and warm. My god, had I pissed myself? I couldn't move. The knees retracted but the blows resumed. My back and shoulders spasmed. My head was twisted to one side. I looked straight into the darkness. It was soft. It folded over my eyeballs. Above me somewhere, someone was screaming. I closed my eyes, opened, closed again. The darkness was inside my skull now, a blooming, black rose. I could see it behind my eyes. I forced them open and then there she was, Calle peering down at me, her red, tumescent face, that New England mom's haircut. She looked right at me. There were welts on her wrists from the restraints we'd put her in. Someone else was screaming, it wasn't her. She stared me in the eye, her lip curled into a smile, and held a finger to her lips. I blinked and she was gone. In my temples, the pounding of many feet. I blinked. There was still someone there, watching me. I saw myself on my belly on the floor, a woman in white floating above me, wet black hair hanging down, a shawl of hair. She was waiting. Her eyes shone. She wore that creamy skin, bare feet.

A sudden, wild yell, followed by groans. Limp weight on my back, pinning me down. Wet. There was a smell.

"Ahhh. Ahhh." A masculine voice, groaning.

Then the weight slowly lifted, allowing my lungs to expand. Someone rolled me over, pulled at my face, shone a light in my eyes. I went blind for a moment. A sound, a word, over and over. It took a minute to recognize my name. My eyes slid away, back toward the woman in white, the breasts beneath her blouse, the black river of hair. But she was gone. I tried to sit up.

"Help," I croaked.

Someone was moaning. I looked around. I'd dropped my flashlight. It was all buried, the dark folded on top of it, a pile of black fur coats.

"I'm here." It was Zosiah. She set the flashlight up on one end and the light reflected off the ceiling, dully illuminating the hall. She was crying. Her face looked small, her eyes squished together. Zosiah wiped at her nose with the back of her hand. "Jesus Christ."

A few feet away lay a body, covered in tar. The source of the moaning. On and on it moaned, pumping out the tar from its side with each gurgling breath. It was sinking into the carpet, making it sticky, the fibers all bunched together. A terrible mess.

The figure flopped forward. Something was sticking out of its side, something shiny, a lever. It was a robot, leaking oil.

"You fucking bitch," the machine said. I knew that voice.

Zosiah was stroking my face. Her hands smelled like blood. She was still crying. She was crying on me. I was starting to put it together.

"What did you do?"

It was Jason, or someone who looked like him. There was a thing sticking out of him, a handle of some sort, which I realized was attached to a knife I could not see because it was inside his body. Zosiah had put it there. Now he was bleeding out, bleeding all over the hallway. I wanted to get up, run, go back to the laundry room and barricade the door. Jason might die, and who knew what he would turn into, what we would all become? Meanwhile, Edison was downstairs, dying, if he hadn't already.

Zosiah threw her arms around me and sobbed into my shoulder. She was talking, a jumble of words I couldn't decipher.

"We have to go." The words came out of my mouth. My brain said, *Get up, get on your feet*, and my muscles did their best to obey. But it was all numb. The pain was there, going somewhere, everywhere, the signals all headed in the wrong direction. Maybe the messages were getting to Jason instead. Maybe he was getting my pain, too and that was part of the groaning. Zosiah helped pull me up. I leaned against her, looked down at the shadow of Jason on the floor. He wasn't getting up. He went on swearing. It no longer seemed to be directed at us. I wasn't sure he even knew we were there.

But as we hobbled off toward the stairs, I heard him again, calling to me, calling my name.

"C'mon . . ." he trailed off. "Don't leave me like this." His voice broke. *It was just a game.*

I stopped. I couldn't see anything. Zosiah was sniffling. Her hands were wet. She smelled like blood and urine and other things I couldn't name.

"Let's go," she whispered.

We hobbled along toward the stairs, Zosiah wielding the flashlight, each step taking us a little farther away from that disembodied voice, floating in the dark, calling "Hey-hey-hey." The door opened, and we pushed through, let it slam behind us, a terrible echo resounding through the stairwell. I shut my eyes against the sound and saw the door closing again on Ruth. She didn't look back.

Now we stood on the landing, the light shining on the steps before us. I could only see a few of them, but I knew the rest were there, too many to count, considering the shape we were in. How were we going to get back?

"What now?"

Zosiah was shaking, but she held onto me tightly. "We'll take it one at a time. Just lean on me. I'll hold you up," she said. "I'll carry you down if I have to."

And she did. She bore me up as we navigated each step, one by one. It took hours, it took days. But the blood on her wasn't her own. I couldn't breathe through my nose. We just had to keep going, down and down and down, as I prayed no more shining faces would emerge from the dark.

XVII

When we got back to the laundry room, Edison was gone. There was just a body on the floor covered up with terrycloth towels, the feet sticking out, the shoes still on. I studied the shape of him beneath the shroud and tried to connect it to the man I had briefly known.

Adrienne knelt beside the body, making flowers out of paper. She had a laundry cart, a big one, the kind I had hidden inside. She looked up when we came in, her expression of surprise quickly turning to confusion, then alarm when she saw the blood, which was on me now, too, and my shredded shirt. It was all over Zosiah, her hands and face and hair. She stank of it. As she helped me lean against one of the washers, Adrienne wet a towel for her but she was shaking too much to hold it, so Adrienne began cleaning up her face for her.

"Is he dead?"

Zosiah shook her head. "He will be." She burst into tears. Then she tossed her hair and began stripping off her clothes. I remembered the tattoo on her buttocks, the constellation.

Orion, the giant. I couldn't make it out in the dim light. But I could see that streak of gray in her hair. It was wide now, a swath of silver that lit up in the gloom, curving out from her face, then drifting down toward her shoulder.

When she was naked, she took the whole bundle of clothes over to the sink and dropped it in. It was too bad the machines wouldn't work. In the cold water, she scrubbed, dunking both hands aggressively into the basin. Adrienne brought her a bar of soap.

Now Adrienne turned to me, gently tried to lift my shirt. I pushed her hands away and she frowned.

"Let me help you."

"No," I croaked but I was too weak to fight her off and eventually she managed to shine her flashlight on my skin. What she saw made her gasp and for a moment I thought it was the sight of me, my body, this skinny container, and shame thrummed through me hot as blood, until I realized it wasn't my chest at all that alarmed her.

"Jesus," she murmured. "You look like you got hit by a bus."

I closed my eyes. I could hear her body moving through space, Zosiah's too, then the sink turning on. Adrienne brought over another towel. It was cool on my face. I opened my eyes. The white towel was dark in her hands.

I didn't ask what had happened to Edison. I knew there was nothing she could tell me that I didn't already know, just as she did not ask me the why or how of Jason, or where Zosiah's purse had gone. I was grateful for that. I saw again the faces in the hallway. The mother's face, the lover, red and swollen, guilty, replaced by the pale, serene visage, so full of sorrow.

Suddenly, I knew who she was, what she wanted from me: she was trapped. The hotel was a vessel. My fingers twitched. I would write it. I would live to write it. I was compelled, a madness, notebooks or no.

Jaime. I shuddered. His voice again. It would follow me. This time, he was behind the glass. The story had begun to write itself. I had to get out, get on with it.

Besides, we were the only ones left.

Zosiah wrung out her clothes and laid them over the machines to dry. Then she wrapped herself in towels: one around her torso, covering most of her thighs, and one over her shoulders, like a cape. She sat shivering atop a washer adjacent to the ones her clothes lay spread across, her bare feet dangling. I wanted to tell her she shouldn't have done it, she'd stopped him and now she'd never be the same, but she looked at me and on her face was a mask I'd never seen her wear. It was done. Now we had to get away.

"We need to go upstairs," I said, and both of them looked at me.

"What?"

"We need to get to a window. We need to look out. Maybe it's gone, maybe it's over." Even as I said it, I knew it was impossible. There was no "over" to this, whatever this was, no matter what was happening outside.

They exchanged glances.

*

I tried to help but couldn't, so together the two of them lifted the shrouded figure, groaning and straining as they went, nearly dropping him, the towels falling away as Zosiah gave up on holding them in place. I looked away. I was afraid his face would haunt me.

They put him in the laundry bin. Adrienne laid the paper flowers on top. Then they wheeled it away while I waited. I didn't want to know where it was going, though I assumed the bin was headed back to the linen closet where they'd leave him, close the door behind them, never open it again. There would be a smell. Rodents and insects would creep in under the door to do their work. By the time that all happened, I told myself, it might not matter.

The room felt cavernous without them. It was cold. I pulled a towel over my shoulders and closed my eyes. I didn't want to see in the dark anymore.

When they came back for me, they said nothing. They had both been crying. It was the first time I'd seen Adrienne like that. Her eyes had shrunk behind her glasses.

"C'mon," she said and handed me my bag with my notebook inside, helped me sling it over my shoulder. Then we went back to the stairs.

It wasn't easier with two of them, as only one at a time could help me, but at least they could take turns. As we climbed, I thought about the blood soaking through the carpet, permeating the floor, the very building embedded with his DNA, and the thought made me want to stop and go back and not take one step closer toward that man up there, or what was left of him, the man who had sat on my back and beaten me into the floor till Zosiah stuck a switchblade in his side to stop him. I shook violently and they thought it was from the cold.

"Almost there," they said, as if that could comfort me. They panted and sweated with their labors, using up their strength.

"Going down was easier," Zosiah admitted, breathless.

When we reached the lobby, we collapsed in a heap onto the floor. Zosiah and Adrienne lay there, gulping for air, too tired to even scan the room.

"Look, look," I said, urging them on, till someone shone a light in the direction of the doors. We were still at the other end of the lobby, yards from the barricade.

Adrienne got up and headed slowly toward the door, holding the light out in front of her like a weapon. By now, dawn had to be on its way. She yanked the sheets down, a great unveiling. They fell with a "woosh" over the tower of furniture. Beyond the glass, there was only an opaque smear of fog mixed with black, an ink drawing. There was nothing there. I thought of Ruth, floating. I shuddered. Adrienne turned off the flashlight.

"Let's go," she said.

"Wait," Zosiah panted. "I need to rest."

"No, let's go." She turned the flashlight back on, pointed its bright pupil at the glass doors. "Let's go now."

I nodded my head, I couldn't speak.

"I'm not going," Zosiah said, but I knew she would follow if Adrienne went first, dragging me along like a giant rag doll, because there was nowhere else to go, we couldn't stay in this tomb.

They set me down, and I lay on the floor as they heaved and pushed the furniture out of the way. I thought about my notebook, the heaviest burden in the smallest of things. Stories lived in me. If I died, would they eek out, like souls?

Finally, the door was uncovered. Adrienne and Zosiah helped me up and I stood propped up between them. We grasped hands.

"I'll go first," Adrienne said.

She unlocked the door. The air rushed in, cold, crisp, carrying a scent of wood smoke. I closed my eyes, let it pass over me, swallowed it down.

Zosiah and Adrienne were taking it in just the same, Zosiah's mouth an 'O,' her eyes pressed closed. We passed over the threshold and all but our clasped hands evaporated as the fog wrapped itself around us like a cloak. Zosiah dug her nails into my palm. There was nothing to see. The bubble of a giggle rose up my throat, the desire to laugh filling me like a gas. Zosiah's hair brushed my face.

"So this is heaven," said a voice, gravelly and French.

The fog shifted, foamy waves rolling apart, rejoining, a dance. There was the street, a car at an angle, its snout biting the curb. Someone was in the car. Frantically, I squeezed Zosiah's hand to make sure it was still there, that I was still there. The person wasn't inside the car but on top of it. I froze. The roof was crushed. I could smell the exhaust and for a moment it was my mother on top of that car. My body convulsed, lurched, curling around a scream, holding it in. But I got no closer, there was nothing to see. The fog swallowed it all up like a memory.

Somewhere, my mother was in her kitchen, crying.

Let's go. I couldn't speak.

Let go.

"What happens now?" Zosiah's whisper a shh in my ear, tongue tickling.

This was a mistake.

There was no going back to the old life. Not for Calle, not for Ruth. Not for us.

"Jaime?"

A weight at my side, the press of flesh. The fog thickened and pulled us close. The hotel had disappeared; there was no hotel. We were lost inside it. There was nothing. All was very still, very quiet.

PART III

I

Duke summons Cly to his office and she finds him scowling at something on his monitor. He motions to her to sit without looking up.

"I heard something upsetting. Do you know what it was?" Now he turns to her, frowning like there's a stench in the room.

She sits there, hands folded into a heart in her lap, unable to speak.

The seconds tick by. "Okay," he sighs. "You're gonna make me say it, then. I heard you were having a relationship with one of our guests, a regular. I heard you went into this person's room. Is that true?"

She inhales sharply. There's a stabbing pain in her chest. Cly has never been a good liar. "For want of practice," she hears her mother say with a smirk in her voice.

"Yes," she says.

Duke sighs again, rubs at his forehead. "I'm trying to understand . . . Okay, you could've at least denied it. It's your word against his, frankly. I didn't actually see any evidence."

"His?"

"Look, you're fired." Duke shrugs. The phone on his desk begins to ring. "I have to fire you, so you're fired." The phone keeps on ringing.

Cly is motionless. It's early, the hotel nearly empty of guests at this hour. Her first check-in isn't scheduled till the afternoon. The phone is still crying, but Duke hasn't picked it up. Finally, it stops.

"Who will take my shift?"

Duke waves the question away. "That's not something you need to worry about now. Look, I'll still be a reference for you. If you want to write yourself a letter of recommendation, I'll sign it for you."

Cly stands up suddenly. The phone starts ringing again.

"I'm sorry, okay? These are the rules. I don't make them!" he calls after her.

Cly doesn't answer. From a great distance, the phone goes silent. Duke says something angrily, then quiets, talking on, the words meaningless. She drifts out of the room, back to the employee locker room, tucked away on a subterranean floor. The light is dim down there, the ceiling low. It flickers as she changes out of her uniform, turning her life on and off, on and off. In her panties, blouse open, Cly sits and puts her head between her knees. She gasps for breath, eyes stinging.

When she's done, she drops the folded uniform in the laundry bin, gently places her earrings and persimmon tree necklace on the shelf above.

Outside she squints against the sunlight, as the wind pulls at her hair. Leaves scuttle past, dancing over her feet.

There are people walking about: tourists with shopping bags, professionals hurrying by, looking straight ahead, their shoes clapping against the pavement. Cly stands there. A few weeks ago, she would've gone to Edith, who's probably at home right now, enjoying her sabbatical. She sucks in her lips. A bolt of anger crackles through her. She doesn't want to think about Edith. She takes a step, then another. Halfway to her stop, she startles, looking around, discovers she's riding the train.

It's not till she's walking home from the station and sticks her hand in her pocket that she realizes she still has her ID, all her keys. She forgot to surrender them, and Duke was so uncomfortable he didn't ask. Cly stops, considers turning around, then finds she has resumed her walk; she's almost at her building.

When she reaches the apartment, no one is there. There's a half-full ashtray on the kitchen table, her mother's notebook next to it, an empty coffee mug on top to hold it closed. The air smells like wilted flowers, mixed with the acrid scent of cigarettes.

Clytemnestra wanders into her parents' tidy bedroom, no sign that anyone has slept there. She wanders out again, heads to the kitchen.

Inside the fridge she finds ketchup and other condiments, a bag of shriveled grapes and a half-empty bottle of white wine, her mother's, long gone sour. The door swings shut, the ancient fridge shudders. A pigeon coos on the windowsill. There are traffic sounds in the distance, a far-away shout—a child, full of delight. At the table, she selects one of Claire's stale cigarettes, lights it, takes a long drag, then looks about the room again. It's

dingy in the natural light, grease coating the stove, the place full
of old smells and papers, books everywhere, stacks of yellowed
mail curling like wood shavings.

Her mother's heavy silver lighter is perched on the table.
She doesn't remember seeing it there yesterday and scans the
room again, half expecting to find Claire sitting in one of the
rickety old chairs, picking a flake of tobacco off the tip of her
tongue, Yorgos hovering over her shoulder like a pet bird,
watching her stare out the window.

Clytemnestra dresses herself in a black silk kimono, one of
her mother's. She doesn't remember hanging it in the closet, or
even having worn it before, but there it is. The sleeves smell like
old roses and smoke.

Then she settles into her father's favorite worn-out chair,
selects one of her mother's books off the nearby shelf. She stares
at the black-and-white author photo on the back cover. Her
mother looks wounded, her lips in a pout, and she's doing
something funny with her hand, like a sideways peace sign. Her
eyes stare straight at the camera, daring it to look back at her.

Supposedly Claire wrote volumes about her many lovers,
but she's never been able to find any of them in her poems,
only herself, the symbol of all regret and disappointment, the
beautiful child weeping in her soiled white underwear, a wet,
chubby hand stuffed in her mouth.

Clytemnestra replaces the book on the shelf, runs her
fingernails over the spines of its neighbors. Somewhere in the
apartment are Yorgos's books, his papers, even his dissertation.
She doesn't bother looking for them. Instead, she picks up a
novel, something long and flowery from another century that

she can lose herself in. But the words won't stay put. Her eyes shift back and forth, letters vanishing, then reappearing somewhere else. They bleed and dribble right off the page. She shuts the book, sets it aside.

When the phone rings, she stares at it and lets it go till the last, insistent cry hangs in the air and dies.

II

Night comes. Clytemnestra watches it steal through the room, how it greedily snatches up patches of sunlight off the floor, bit by bit. At last, the room is black and still. Outside, a siren shrieks uncontrollably. She listens, waits.

In the bathroom, a face is there, waiting for her in the mirror above the sink, a purple mark on the forehead, red at the center, an angry third eye. Her stare has gone hard, the mouth sour.

There's something behind the mirror: a secret compartment full of vials, slick tubes, and amber bottles that rattle with tiny white pills like chips of bone. There's a gold tube of lipstick as well. The face returns, smiles demurely now. Clytemnestra paints the mouth a deep, creamy red. The light goes off and the face disappears. The mirror gleams, silver, flashing a shard, pointed as a tooth.

She dresses herself in a white peasant blouse and a matching skirt that's long, loose, and nearly covers her feet. They're Claire's clothes, leftover from her youth, back when she would've worn white without thinking, the underarms yellowed from old sweat, those deodorant-less days. They've been in this closet longer than she's been alive. She puts on a fur-lined coat from decades later, too warm for the season. She stuffs the pockets with the keys, the ID card, her mother's lighter and cigarettes.

She travels unseen; no one looks at her on the street, on the subway. The artificial light washes everything in a pall of neon urine. It flickers, goes out for a moment. They pass through a black tunnel. The train clatters and roars, the wheels shriek and give off sparks that skitter into the dark. Then the train screeches, lurches to a stop. She drifts through the narrow, subterranean hall, then up the stairs, into the world. Already the hem of her skirt is soiled.

Cabs pass, honking. Couples go by, arm in arm, talking to each other in low voices, laughing, their heads thrown back, teeth bared. A woman alone with many bags, another with just an umbrella. A pack of kids rushes past, whooping and hollering at the moon, a chalky white pie.

It's there at the end of the block: small, white, unobtrusive, almost humble, like a church, the doors made of tinted glass. They're shut. You can't see into the lobby from the outside. It looks dark in there, closed up. For a moment, she hesitates. Something is different. Her feet carry her closer. She slips past the front, goes around the corner, then through the staff entrance. The key card still works. She glides through the hall till she reaches the stairs, passes the card over the sensor. It beeps, flashes: denied. She tries again. Another failure. Her hands shake.

The door swings open before a man in a maintenance jumper, not one of the hotel's uniforms. Maybe he belongs to an external clean-up crew. He looks her over, smiles. He's big-nosed, handsome, with soft, black curls, like her father. She returns the smile, and he holds the door for her. As she moves past him, their bodies brush against each other.

The doorway to the ninth floor is taped off, plastic sashes read "Do Not Enter." She takes them down, lays them on the carpet. The ninth floor is quiet, dim, the only light emanating from the little bulbs above each doorway. She looks around for tools, building materials, piles of sawdust, or debris and finds nothing but some planks of wood and skeins of black wires. Sheets of plastic cover the floor and each of the doors.

Carefully, she lifts the plastic, tries a handle. It clicks, the door slowly opens. The light coming through the window is enough to see by. She takes off her coat and lays it on the bed. Then she sets her shoes by the door. At the window, she stands invisible, studying the patterns of lights flashing below, trying to decipher their signals.

She can't sleep, paces the length of the hall, the plastic tarps crinkling. She peels the sheets away like old skin so she can feel the carpet beneath her feet, rubs her toes in it, digs in deep. It's so clean and soft. Clytemnestra lies flat on the floor, holding an unlit cigarette, mimes the in- and exhale. She won't pollute this space with actual cigarette smoke.

"So this is heaven." Claire smirks.

It's the floor in-between, she explains. It is part of the hotel, and yet it is also separate, which is why it's always deserted.

"You look like a bride," her mother says. It is neither a compliment nor an insult. She understands this implicitly.

People always misinterpret things her mother says, get confused by her accent, her mocking smile. They laugh at jokes that are not jokes. They are frightened of her.

"What will you do up here?" Her mother wants her to go home. The hotel, always complaints about the hotel, as if it were a prison of some sort and not a sanctuary.

"The world should be harsh. It's foolish to demand otherwise."

"This is home, Maman."

Her mother scoffs.

She thinks of the guests above and below, tucked away in their rooms. What if you could hear them? The hum of their grief, a chorus of wails. It would shatter the stillness, overwhelm the walls. It would stop traffic on the street outside. Pedestrians would pause, alarmed, and look around, awaiting disaster. And when none came—no walls crumbling, no clouds of smoke, no blood spattered on the pavement—when no sirens sounded, they would think they had imagined it, that their own suffering had manifested into a terrible song of grief.

*

Clytemnestra dreams she's at home. Her mother sits with her leg slung over the arm of her chair, the knee the widest part of it, the place where the bone swells. *J'ai des beaux os*, writes Anne Hébert, but she's Canadian, not French, so what does she know? Behind her, the books stand angled into uneven towers like ancient vertebrae, spiraling upward to graze the ceiling. The towers sway. Remove one and the whole thing will topple.

Where are the bookshelves? she wonders. Why are the books stacked like this, the first one touching the floor? Her father says it's a sin to let books touch the ground, even though he doesn't believe in God. Where is her father?

She turns to her mother. There's a smear of lipstick across her mouth, a gash from chin to nose, red paste in the lines that frame her lips, the ones that have deepened over time from too much smoking. She's smoking now, the cigarette stained red. Her fingertips match.

"Where's Papa?"

Claire nods, points her cigarette at her daughter. "He'll be along shortly."

Behind her, a wall of glass, the whole island outlined below, tiny and self-contained as a snow globe. What floor are they on? Clytemnestra doesn't remember being this high up before. She realizes she's barefoot and wearing a white skirt, which clings to her legs in the wind. There is no glass; the window frame is empty.

Her mother studies her, eyes narrowed, sucking on her cigarette. There are little dabs of lipstick all over her face, red half-moons under her eyes, a slash across her forehead.

"Why don't you sit down? Why don't you rest for a minute?"

Clytemnestra looks around, searching for the door. She can't find it. The room has grown round, endless. There's no entryway for her father to pass through.

Claire shakes her head. "Always going in the wrong direction."

"Where's Papa?"

Her mother rolls her eyes. "I told you, he'll be along shortly."

"You're always keeping him to yourself."

Her mother's eyes grow frighteningly wide. She leans forward, slams the flat of her palm against the table. "What?"

"Nothing."

Claire leans back, lights another cigarette.

"He killed himself for you."

She scoffs. "Your father isn't dead. He isn't any deader than I."

"But you're dead, too."

Claire pauses, considering this. "Oh." She shrugs.

Clytemnestra shakes her head. Tears stream down her face. "That was not enough. That was never enough for him. The poor man. He loved you."

Claire fiddles with her lighter. She flips it open and closed, stares into the flame, blows on it. It doesn't bend. "He'll be along shortly."

"I don't want to be here with you."

Her mother looks up, surprised.

Clytemnestra wakes up, gasping. There's a pillow over her face; she throws it to the floor. For a moment she doesn't remember where she is. Then: *her* floor. Her skirt is twisted around her waist and legs. She tears at it, panting, and claws her own skin. Tears and snot cover her lips.

There's a tap at the door. Startled, she looks up. No, it can't be. The room is soundproof. Is she still in the dream? She remembers the defeat on her father's face, there in the hallway outside the room her mother died in. She blinks hard. Before her eyes, a flash of Edith, that wry smile. Then Edith on her knees in her daughter's room, her face buried in the bed's pink coverlet.

At the clinic upstate they liked to call a spa, they hooked Claire up to an IV, tied her down, forced things into her throat. Clytemnestra wasn't there yet. She had to work. Her father whispered into the phone. She put a hand over her mouth so he wouldn't know she was crying.

He was in the room with her when Clytemnestra arrived because Claire was too weak to kick him out. She didn't look like herself. She was transforming before their eyes. Her father sat hunched over, elbows on his knees, head in his hands, fingers stuck in his thick black curls. They had a chair for him, but not for her. Her mother was sedated, her father explained. When she woke, her eyes would go wild and she'd try to pull out all the tubes, rip off the oxygen mask. Clytemnestra leaned against the wall, put a hand on her father's shoulder, and cried silently. It had all happened too fast to be believed.

As if hearing her thoughts, Yorgos cried out, "How could this happen?"

She didn't know what to say. Her whole life, her mother had never been well, not really. She had always been too thin, weak. That was just the way she was. It seemed she would go on like that forever. Claire was too fierce to die, had outlived too many other poets—those gentle, malleable souls.

She is just one person, Clytemnestra longed to wrap her father in these words. He was so impossibly small. *She was only flesh, the same as you.* The power of that one person to arrest your breath, to shock you sick at the sight of her, a seizing of your heart. The force of that woman, like an act of God, or Nature.

The grief was there next to him, a thing she couldn't see but felt. In a second, it lunged out of the dark, swallowed him whole.

It wasn't surprise she felt when she came home from work and found him with a silk sash around his neck, it was only rage and a loneliness so deep, she can never climb out of it.

It was a silk tie from one of her mother's robes. White, with a pattern of painted red and gold flowers. Old but well-preserved. Pristine. He tied it to a doorknob.

She called an ambulance. Then she stood over him, looking down at his waxen face, his soft hair. Just last night he'd cooked her dinner before her late shift at the hotel. He struggled to smile as she ate, consumed nothing himself. His eyes watered constantly.

Clytemnestra took his hand, pressed his fingers to her palm. "She didn't deserve you."

At the funeral, former colleagues who hadn't spoken to him since he left the university in disgrace came up to her, put their hands on her arm.

"He was a good man, a good teacher."

She nodded at them. He was a good many things.

From inside her skull, her mother peeked out, observing, wearing a hat with a raven's head on top. She scoffed at their ersatz tears, the waving hankies.

"Where were they then?" she demanded, as if they could've saved him, saved Claire. Clytemnestra's mouth tasted of ash.

*

She opens the door, peers into the hall. Silence. She's about to close it again when something catches her eye, a black blemish embedded in the carpet. It's a long-limbed insect, thin as thread. She bends down. It isn't an insect at all but a tiny strip of wires attached to a plastic head. Cly gently pinches the thing between two fingers and brings it up to her face. It's a camera. So small, once installed, it will be nearly invisible. For a moment, the object seems so foreign, she cannot imagine what it's doing there.

"It's your word against his," Duke said. She surveys the parallel rows of doors leading down the hall. The rumor, cameras in the rooms. Who saw her in the room with Edith? She sucks in her breath. They—the unseen—see everything. Room after room, floor upon floor. Row upon row of eyes. A wave of nausea hits her, knocks her over.

"I never say 'I told you so,' though I did." Claire says. "What does private mean in a public place, hm?" she ponders, hooking her fingers around the word "private." Surely, she would know best. Even her poetry was a theater, one she didn't have to be present to act out. People took it home with them, wrote essays and dissertations they published in turn.

Clytemnestra kneels. The camera is still in her hand. It's smaller than her fingernail. She flicks it out of her palm and it flies up toward the ceiling. For a moment it really is alive, flying, till it descends in an arc, disappears, buried in the fibers of the carpet. It's gone. But she can't unsee it. She scans the doors again, one after the other. They aren't portals. No one is healed. *Someone died here.* Clytemnestra leans over her knees, braces her hands against the floor. More people will kill themselves and they know it, so they're keeping an eye on them. Perhaps they can see her right now.

"Then why haven't they come to remove you?" Claire wonders.

Clytemnestra returns to the room, throws the door shut but it's on a tightly coiled hinge and closes slowly, apologizing for itself. She sits on the bed and looks around the room. There is still so much breakable glass. And then it's there, like a door she never noticed before: she contemplates a bath, the rose-colored water. It would be a long time before anyone found her. She shudders. Macabre stories would be published about her, her parents.

And if she's gone, whose head will her mother live inside?

Clytemnestra doubles over again and cries.

When she's finished, she lights one of her stale cigarettes and lets the smoke sniff its way around the upholstery and linens, feel up the drapes. Ash falls over the floor and with her bare feet she rubs it deep into the carpet. The smell of the smoke is chemical, sour, entirely out of place. Still, when the first burns down, she uses the end to light another and it glows with possibility. Clytemnestra lies down on the bed, ash drifting over the white duvet, and watches the cigarette consume itself steadily, not knowing it'll reach an end.

She wakes, choking. A fog has settled in the room. It presses against the window, envelopes the bed. The bed is on fire. Clytemnestra rolls to the floor, pulling the sheets down with her, the flames muffled for a moment by the heap, till they eek out, glowing bright with hunger, chewing the black, curling hem of the blanket. She scrambles to her feet and flees, only to find the smoke follows her into the hallway. She covers her mouth, hunches over, coughing. Her throat is raw.

"This is not how you burn down a building," her mother laughs. "This is how you choke. Is that what you want?"

Clytemnestra ignores her, keeps moving toward the farthest end of the hall.

Her mother cackles in her ear. "You're an artist now, my dear."

There's a "click," then suddenly water is pouring from the ceiling, torrential as a monsoon, spraying the bed, the hallway, streaming down the walls. The lights short out as the carpet turns to marsh. A black river streams through her hair, down over her shoulders and breasts, dissolving her white clothes. Behind her, peering over her shoulder, Claire shakes her head.

It's raining in the hotel. Clytemnestra cups her palms to catch it. There are cameras. This life is absurd, more horrifying than anything she could've imagined. She laughs. It squeezes its way out of her, a foreign body. In this moment, anything is possible.

Then, just like that, the rain stops.

Her skirt swabs the stairs as she slowly takes the nine flights down to exit through a side door. An alarm should sound but doesn't. When she reaches the street, she finds an ambulance, a cluster of uniformed employees holding their sides, studying the pavement.

Duke is in the crowd looking wan, frightened. They lock eyes, and she freezes. She's been caught. His eyes flicker, land on something else. No, he doesn't recognize her like this.

There are police cars around the ambulance, sirens off, the cops standing solemnly by, no guns drawn. Suddenly, the doors to the lobby burst open and real EMTs roll out a stretcher with a black bag strapped to it. They move slowly, one of the wheels ticks.

It's happening now: there's a body rolling out of the hotel. She scans the crowd. They're watching, covering their mouths. No one sees her, she isn't there.

Claire emerges to take in the scene. "Oh, merde."

Someone is dead, cameras or no. As if they heard her, took their own rose-colored bath, flesh soft and wrinkled as an overripe peach, red on the inside. Who? Who checked them in?

A man in coveralls rushes up to Duke, who tosses his head at him like a bull. "Do I have to explain what triage means to you?" He waves him off, disgusted.

The man slouches, crosses his arms. He's familiar; he held the door and let her back in, violating protocol.

He sees her and gives her a quick upward nod with his chin. He knows her. A grin. Cold fingers creep over her body. He's staring at her.

They load the corpse into the ambulance and shut the doors.

Clytemnestra pushes through the crowd, struggling to reach Duke. Her clothes are heavy, the skirt inching down her hips. Someone steps on the hem and it tears.

"Who is it?" she's breathless, her voice barely audible.

"What?" Duke scowls, confused. He looks her over. "Who—Clytemnestra?"

"Who was it?" She turns, points. The ambulance is leaving.

"What the fuck are you doing here?" He tilts his head back and sighs. "Jesus Christ. What a day."

"Please," Clytemnestra breathes. "Just tell me, who was it? Was it a woman?"

Duke pulls a ringing cell phone out of his pocket. "Hello?" he glares at her, mouths "go away," then turns his back to her.

The man in the coveralls appears at her side. "Hey, you all right?" There's a touch of Jersey in his voice.

"Do you know who it was?"

He shakes his head. "Some lady. She had this knife on her, like a sword." He holds his hands out to measure it. He shakes his head again as he looks her up and down. "You know the weird thing?" He leans in. "She had a cat with her."

Edith doesn't have a cat, or a sword. She's alive somewhere, or, at least, not dead here, and that's enough.

Clytemnestra eyes the man beside her. "How do you know all this?"

He stiffens. "Just what I heard."

The crowd parts for Duke. He's glowering, heading straight at her. She turns away from the man, from the hotel where a woman was just removed in a plastic bag, and rushes toward the street, then the train that will ferry her uptown.

"So, now what?"

Clytemnestra is halfway down the subway steps when she stops. Someone behind her bumps her shoulder, then the man turns to give her a dirty look as he passes by, stirring the air. She's soaked and smells like fire. She's hurrying back to an empty apartment, full of her parents' relics and writings. What for? I don't exist, she thinks. Without the hotel, I'm nothing, no one.

Claire frowns, waves her hand. "Nonsense," she declares. "This is where you begin."

ACKNOWLEDGEMENTS

With thanks:

To my hobbit-love and bestest beta reader Jensen Sikora, who taught me what it's like to live with magic every day.

To my mother Cindy Pacini for her boundless pride and love over many years of struggle to bring this book to life.

To Brooke Stevens who's been my champion and guide since I was eighteen and first entered his classroom at Sarah Lawrence. Thank you for always believing in me and providing a kind word every time I nearly succumbed to writerly despair.

To Sarah Lawrence professor and Director of the Brooklyn College MFA Fiction program Josh Henkin, as well as the entire Brooklyn MFA faculty, in particular Michael Cunningham, Mary Morris, Sapphire, and Ernesto Mestre-Reed. Each of you in your own way nudged me toward becoming the writer I was meant to be. Thank you for your wisdom and guidance.

A warm, bourbon-rich note of love and gratitude to my dear friend, song sister, and editor extraordinaire Deborah Steinberg, who first recognized my vision and helped put the pieces of this manuscript together. Thank you for your patience, vision, and support.

I am grateful to Amanda Manns and Olivia Batker Pritzker, champions of feminist literature and the founders of Creature Publishing, whose keen insight took this story to new emotional heights. Thank you for midwifing this book into the world.

To my agent Kate Garrick who believed in this novel from the start and has stood by me throughout the highs and lows of this incredible journey. Cheers to you!

To all the wild women of Conspiracy of Venus who welcomed me and taught me their songs so I could find my voice again.

To all the bosses who never noticed I was writing at my desk. I appreciate your negligence . . . I mean . . . trust.

Last but not least, a special thank you to Elsie Maris Merbaum, the embodiment of unconditional love. I never doubt you're always with me.

LINDSAY MERBAUM is a queer feminist author and high priestess of home mixology. After graduating from Sarah Lawrence College, she earned her MFA in Fiction from Brooklyn College, where she was a recipient of the Himan Brown Award. Her award-nominated short fiction has appeared in *PANK*, Anomalous Press, The Collagist, *Epiphany*, *Gargoyle*, Day One, *Harpur Palate*, and *Hobart*, among others. Her essays and interviews can also be found in Electric Literature, Bustle, Bitch Media, The Rumpus, and more. Lindsay lives in Michigan with her partner and cats and serves as an editor of book reviews at Necessary Fiction. *The Gold Persimmon* is her first novel.

CREATURE PUBLISHING was founded on a passion for feminist discourse and horror's potential for social commentary and catharsis. Seeking to address the gender imbalance and lack of diversity traditionally found in the horror genre, Creature is a platform for stories which challenge the status quo. Our definition of feminist horror, broad and inclusive, expands the scope of what horror can be and who can make it.

CPSIA information can be obtained
at www.ICGtesting.com
Printed in the USA
LVHW092046011021
699218LV00006B/8